THE BOBBSEY TWINS'
BIG ADVENTURE AT HOME

The Bobbsey Twins'

Big Adventure at Home

By

LAURA LEE HOPE

GROSSET & DUNLAP

Publishers • New York

Published in 2004 by Grosset & Dunlap, a division of Penguin Young
Readers Group, 345 Hudson Street, New York, New York 10014.
GROSSET & DUNLAP is a trademark of Penguin Group (USA) Inc.
THE BOBBSEY TWINS® is a registered trademark of
Simon & Schuster, Inc.

Printed in the U.S.A.

ISBN 0-448-43759-7

1 3 5 7 9 10 8 6 4 2

CONTENTS

CHAPTER I

A PIRATE GAME

BERT Bobbsey rushed down the aisle of the train and stopped where his twin sister was seated.

"Nan," he whispered, "there's a savage dog in the baggage car. A trunk fell against his crate and broke some of the slats. I'm afraid he'll get out and hurt our Snap."

Instantly the slim, brown-haired girl jumped up. "Oh, Bert! How awful!" she cried, immediately fearful for their pet dog's safety.

The brother and sister, twelve years old, turned to their mother, who sat reading across the aisle.

"Is something wrong?" asked pretty Mrs. Bobbsey, seeing her children's worried expressions.

Quickly Bert explained. "May we run back and make sure Snap will be safe?"

"Very well. But I'm sure the baggage attendant won't let anything happen," Mrs. Bobbsey said.

"He's not there now," Bert told her.

At this moment a voice piped up, "Please let Flossie and me go, too!"

A chubby boy and girl of six with blond hair and big blue eyes scrambled from their seat in front of Mrs. Bobbsey and stood with Bert and Nan.

"Yes, Freddie and I want to help save Snap!" declared the little girl, tossing her curls.

Mrs. Bobbsey smiled at her younger son and daughter, who also were twins. "All right. But you must stay close to Bert and Nan."

Freddie and Flossie promised they would, and the four Bobbseys started toward the baggage car. Just then someone behind them said:

"Please—do you mind if I go with you?"

The children stopped and turned around. The person who had spoken was a slender, sun-tanned boy about two years older than Bert.

"My name is Jimmy Dodge," he said. "I heard you talking about the mean dog. I'm worried about Laddie, my dog. He's in the baggage car, too."

"Sure. Come along," replied Bert with a smile. He introduced himself and his brother and sisters.

"Two sets of twins!" Jimmy exclaimed as he

and the Bobbseys walked through the cars. "You must have lots of fun!"

"Oh, we do," Flossie assured him "We're always having 'ventures."

Jimmy smiled, but Nan thought he had a sad look in his eyes, nevertheless. By now the five had reached the door of the baggage car. Bert, who was in the lead, entered and the others crowded in behind him. Such an uproar!

Dogs were barking and yelping, cats were meowing and hissing, and there was even a parrot, squawking loudly in his cage. Anxiously the twins and Jimmy Dodge looked about for their own pets.

"There's Snap!" Freddie cried, pointing to a large, shaggy-haired dog with great brown eyes. On seeing his "family," he barked excitedly and pressed his nose against the wooden slats of his crate.

Jimmy spotted his Laddie, a lovely young collie. The pup was near Snap. Both dogs wagged their tails furiously.

"Where's the bad dog?" Freddie asked Bert.

His brother pointed to a crate in between Laddie and Snap. The animal inside it was thin, and his black coat matted. He was growling and thrusting his head through the space left by the broken slats.

The twins and Jimmy looked frantically for the attendant. He was not in sight. The black dog continued trying to force his way free.

"Oh dear!" Nan exclaimed. "What'll we do?"

Flossie started forward. She wanted to tell Snap not to be afraid and that pretty soon he'd be safely in Lakeport.

"Flossie! Look out!" Bert shouted above the din. Nan raced after Flossie and grasped her by the hand. She pulled her back just as the unfriendly dog, with a snarl, squeezed halfway out of his crate. He glared fiercely at the two girls.

"Ooh!" Flossie shuddered as she retreated backward with her sister. "He—he's going to come after us!"

Just then a large, rugged-looking man in a uniform entered the baggage car. "What's going on here?" he demanded in a booming voice.

"Are you the man who takes care of the animals?" Freddie asked him promptly.

"Yes, I am. What can I do for you children?"

Flossie spoke up. "That black dog is getting out!"

The man took one look at the animal, who was almost out of his crate, and leaped forward.

"Boy! He's not afraid at all," Jimmy remarked admiringly.

The children watched the attendant push the growling dog firmly back into the box. He called back, "Don't worry. I'll nail this crate up again in a jiffy."

Reassured, the Bobbseys and Jimmy thanked

the man. He gave them a friendly wave, and the children walked back to their coach.

"Why don't you and your family come sit with us?" Bert invited Jimmy.

The other boy was silent for a moment, then said, "I'd like to very much. I'm traveling alone. My—my family isn't here."

Nan felt sure now that Jimmy was sad about something. He had a wistful look on his face. By now the little group had reached Mrs. Bobbsey.

"Snap's all right," Freddie reported importantly. "Laddie is, too. The baggage man won't let the mean dog bother them."

"That's fine, dear." Mrs. Bobbsey smiled. "Is Laddie a new chum of Snap's?"

"Yes," Flossie put in. "And this is Jimmy Dodge. He's our new friend, and Laddie belongs to him."

"Jimmy's alone on the train," Nan explained, "so he's going to sit with us."

"I'm glad to meet you, Jimmy," Mrs. Bobbsey said warmly. "Are you going far?"

"No, ma'am. Just to Lakeport."

"Lakeport!" Freddie echoed. "That's where we live."

Jimmy's face lit up. "Say, that's swell! Because we—Grandma and I—have just moved there from Belleville."

"Do you live with your grandmother?" inquired Mrs. Bobbsey gently. She too had detected an air of sadness about Jimmy.

"Yes. Grandma is all the family I have now. My mother died a long time ago, and my father —" Jimmy's voice broke a little, "my father was lost at sea. He was captain of the freighter *Flying Dolphin*. It was wrecked in a storm off the Pacific coast of South America."

"Oh, how terrible!" Nan murmured. No wonder Jimmy seemed sad.

Flossie asked in a soft voice, "And your daddy didn't come home?"

Jimmy nodded gravely. "Grandma and I

were told that some of the crew were rescued, but Dad was never found."

The twins were so intent on listening to the lad's story that they remained standing around him. Mrs. Bobbsey leaned forward and said hopefully:

"Perhaps, Jimmy, your father managed to get aboard a lifeboat and landed safely somewhere."

"I'll bet he did," Bert put in, "and drifted to an island way out in the ocean."

Jimmy brightened a little. "That's what Grandma and I keep hoping, because one of the lifeboats was missing." He sighed. "If Dad were alive, though, I'm sure he'd have let us know by now. The *Flying Dolphin* was wrecked a year and a half ago."

"Maybe," Flossie said, "your daddy's on an island that doesn't have any mailboxes and he can't send a letter."

This made everyone chuckle, and Jimmy looked more cheerful. "Anyhow," he said, "I feel luckier since I met you Bobbseys."

Bert grinned. "Say, will you be going to Junior High this fall? That's near our school."

Jimmy nodded. "I hope I can find a job before school starts. If I earn a little money, it'll help my grandmother. She works as a dressmaker at a shop in Lakeport. A friend told her about it, and that's why she decided to move. You see, the insurance company won't send any money to her till it's proved my father is dead."

Nan looked thoughtful. Then she said to her mother, "Daddy might have some part-time work for Jimmy at the lumberyard."

Mr. Richard Bobbsey owned a large lumber business in Lakeport. It was situated on the shores of beautiful Lake Metoka.

"That's a splendid idea," replied Mrs. Bobbsey, smiling. "We'll ask your father when he meets us at the station."

Jimmy beamed in delight, then Freddie said, "Boy, I hope Dinah has something good for supper at home. I sure am hungry."

Dinah Johnson was the plump, jolly woman who helped Mrs. Bobbsey with the cooking and housework. Her husband Sam drove one of the lumberyard trucks. The couple had lived for years in rooms on the third floor of the Bobbsey home and were beloved by the family.

"I'm hungry, too," Flossie declared.

Mrs. Bobbsey chuckled. "Well, you children won't have long to wait, but I'll give you each an apple from Meadowbrook Farm."

"Mmm," Nan said, biting into hers. "Meadowbrook apples are the best."

"Is that where you stayed this summer?" Jimmy guessed.

"Yes," Bert replied. "The farm belongs to our aunt and uncle. It's a swell place."

Jimmy said that he, too, was returning from a farm, which was located in another state. "Dad and Grandma and I used to live there, before we went to Belleville. This summer Mr. Hobbs, the new owner, let me work there. He gave me the collie. I hope Grandma will like Laddie as much as I do."

"Oh, she will!" exclaimed Flossie, turning around, "Laddie's a bee-yoo-ti-ful puppy."

"And he's smart, too," Jimmy said. "I'll bet he'll help me find my buried treasure."

"Buried treasure!" all four twins echoed excitedly, and Freddie burst out, "You mean, like pirates' buried treasure?"

"Almost," replied Jimmy.

"Oh, please tell us about it," Flossie begged.

Jimmy smiled. "Each year after my mother died, Dad tried to be home on my birthday. We'd dress up like pirates and go to an island near Belleville. It's on Lake Metoka, just as Lakeport is. Dad would bury some special treasure for me in an iron box. On my twelfth birthday he was at sea, but he buried my treasure for that year on a Pacific island off South America."

"How exciting!" Nan remarked.

"My father," Jimmy went on, "promised we would take a trip there on my eighteenth birthday to get that treasure, since it was the last one and also much more valuable than the others."

Flossie's eyes were round as silver dollars.

"Haven't you found any of the treasures?" she asked Jimmy.

The boy shook his head. "Not yet! The first treasure, which Dad buried on my seventh birthday, was to be 'discovered' on my thirteenth. And the same idea after that, every year for six years."

"Ooh!" squealed Flossie. "What a wonderful birthday present!"

"Yes. Only," Jimmy continued sadly, "my father was lost just before my thirteenth birthday, so I didn't start looking then. But now Grandma says Dad would want me to go ahead and hunt for the first one. I have a key for each box."

With a puzzled look, Nan asked, "But if you were with your father, don't you remember where the boxes are hidden?"

Jimmy smiled. "Part of our pirate game," he explained, "was for me to put on a blindfold when Dad buried the treasures. So I don't know what's in the boxes or where he hid them. He's the only one in the world who knew."

"You mean," Flossie put in, "you'll have to dig up every island near here?"

This made Jimmy chuckle. "Maybe, if I can't find the charts Dad made. There are lots of little islands in Lake Metoka, you know."

At the Bobbseys' questioning looks, he became serious. "My father drew swell charts for each buried treasure, just like the old-time pirate maps. They're marked I, II, III, etc., and each one has a different code in numbers."

"You mean," Bert asked, "you could figure out from the code the right place to hunt?"

"Yes," replied Jimmy. "Dad showed the maps to me before he went away on his last trip, and he mailed me the one for the Pacific island treasure. He was going to explain the codes to me when he got back."

"Oh dear," Flossie said. "Are the pirate maps lost?"

"I'm afraid so," Jimmy replied. "Grandma wrote me and said the packet of charts has been missing ever since she moved to Lakeport. She hasn't been able to look much, but I want to as soon as I get home."

The Bobbseys were silent for a moment, pondering Jimmy's problem. Then Freddie asked eagerly, "Can we help you hunt for the maps—"

"And figure out where the treasures are?" Flossie broke in, clapping her hands.

"We'd like to," Bert added eagerly.

Jimmy's face shone. "That'd be neat! And would you come with me to look for the treasures, too?"

"Oh, yes!" Nan spoke up, her eyes sparkling.

The twins and their new friend began to discuss plans for the search. Presently Bert became aware that someone else appeared very much interested in their conversation.

A man across the aisle from the Bobbseys had moved to the edge of his seat and cocked his head as if listening intently. He wore his hat pulled low over his forehead. Bert noted that the man had a long, jagged scar across his right cheek. He kept staring at Jimmy Dodge.

Before Bert could inform the others of the man's interest, the train screeched to an abrupt halt. The next moment Freddie cried out:

"Wow! There are some hold-up men right outside our window!"

CHAPTER II

A CHASE

EVERYONE rushed to the train windows. The twins were startled by the sight outside. Fierce-looking masked men wearing red bandannas were milling about. Clustered nearby were women in lovely silk gowns with hoop skirts, and men in high-crowned black hats.

The Bobbseys and Jimmy Dodge and the other passengers stared at the scene in astonishment. Just then the conductor came by.

Freddie tugged at his sleeve. "Are—are those bad men going to rob our train?" he asked.

The conductor grinned. "No. What you see is a movie in the making about a train robbery in olden days. We've been carrying a special engine for them to use. It has just been unhitched."

He pointed to four old-style railroad cars on another track. "That's going to be the next

13

scene. The crew will shoot it as soon as the engine's hooked on."

Flossie clapped her hands excitedly. "Oh, may we get off and watch?" she begged.

"Sure. Go ahead."

Jimmy and the Bobbseys hurried outside into the warm, late afternoon sunshine. They watched in fascination as the "movie" engine was coupled to the four old-fashioned cars. Then the director, a tall man wearing a green beret, signaled the actors to take their places.

"Camera! Action!" he shouted.

Instantly the "robbers" swarmed aboard the held-up train. The ladies in the silk costumes peered in terror from the windows. The tall-hatted men began fighting the masked bandits.

Freddie forgot he was watching a make-believe robbery. The little boy wanted to help defend the train. The next second he darted forward and raced toward the movie set.

Mrs. Bobbsey gasped. "Oh! Freddie will ruin the scene!"

But at that moment the director shouted, "Cut!" and the camera stopped whirring. The man in the green beret strode over to Freddie, who now looked very frightened.

"So! You wanted to steal the scene!" roared the director, towering above the little boy.

"Oh, no," Freddie quavered. "I—I didn't want to steal anything. I just wanted to fight the bad men."

To his surprise the director threw back his head and laughed heartily. Everyone else did, too—actors, actresses, and onlookers.

"You mean I didn't hurt the picture?" Freddie asked.

"Not a bit," the director replied. "The camera stopped in time." The man's eyes twinkled. "If audiences think this movie is as real as you did, it'll be a smash hit—or my name isn't Jay Roland."

Freddie was thrilled when Mr. Roland walked back with him to his family and Jimmy. After introductions were made, Mrs. Bobbsey apologized for her small son.

"No harm done," the director assured her. "I hope you and the twins will come to see my picture when it reaches your home-town theater."

"We will," Flossie promised with a giggle. " 'Specially because Freddie was almost in it."

The rest of the scene was shot without interruption. The travelers boarded their train once more, and it started off.

"Boy!" Jimmy exclaimed, "I can see why Flossie says you're always having adventures!"

The Bobbseys laughed, and Bert said, "Our next one will be helping you look for your pirate treasures."

Flossie sighed. "I wish we were in Lakeport and could start hunting right now."

"Me too," Freddie declared. "And after we find the treasures buried on islands around here, Jimmy, we could go dig up the box your daddy hid on the Pacific Ocean island."

"Oh, Freddie," said his twin scornfully, "how would we ever get there? It's *millions* of miles away."

Mrs. Bobbsey smiled. "Not that far, honey. But it is a long way from here."

Freddie was not discouraged. "I'll bet Daddy could build us a boat," he said firmly. "And it'll have a pirate flag on it, too."

Jimmy then told the Bobbseys about some of his father's former voyages. "Many times," the boy said, "Dad's ship was at the very spot where pirates raided Spanish ships called galleons, loaded with gold, hundreds of years ago."

"How exciting!" Nan exclaimed. "What place is that, Jimmy?"

"Along the coast of South America. The galleons would pick up gold from the mines there and carry it first to Panama, then across the ocean to Manila. But the pirates often waited in boats offshore and attacked the gold ships before they got very far."

At this moment Bert, who sat with Nan facing Jimmy, caught sight of the scar-faced man again. This time the stranger was standing by his seat holding a cup of water. But he was not drinking it.

Instead, he was staring at Jimmy, obviously listening to what the boy was saying.

"Next stop Lakeport!" the conductor shouted just then.

In the scramble to gather up suitcases Bert temporarily forgot about the curious stranger. Now the Bobbsey twins watched eagerly from the windows for a glimpse of their father. The train rolled to a stop. The Bobbseys, accompanied by Jimmy, hastened onto the platform.

"Daddy!" Flossie shrieked in delight. She ran to meet a tall, handsome man coming toward them.

"And Dinah!" cried Freddie. With Mr. Bobbsey was a beaming woman who evidently had been marketing.

There was a joyful reunion as the twins' father kissed his family. "Seems like a long time since I left you at Meadowbrook, instead of only a few days ago," Mr. Bobbsey said.

"It's sure been powerful quiet around home," declared Dinah.

Suddenly Flossie squealed, "Oh, Dinah, you've brought Snoop to meet us!"

In the cook's arms snuggled a black cat with a white chin. "Old Snoop's missed you all, too," said Dinah. "Where's Snap?"

"In the baggage car." Bert turned to Jimmy, who had hung back a little. "Dad and Dinah, this is Jimmy Dodge. He has a dog in the car, too. We'll get Snap and Laddie uncrated now. The train will be pulling out soon."

The two boys went off to reclaim their pets. Freddie looked worried. "I hope that mean black dog won't escape again."

Mrs. Bobbsey explained to her husband about the belligerent animal.

"In that case," he said, "we'd better see how Bert and Jimmy are making out."

Dinah stayed to watch the luggage, and the family walked toward the baggage car. Flossie carried Snoop, who was purring loudly. Nan took her father's arm and quickly told him about Jimmy Dodge and why he had moved to Lakeport.

"He wants to earn some money to help his

grandmother," the girl concluded. "Would you have some work Jimmy could do at the lumberyard, Dad?"

Mr. Bobbsey answered with a smile, "I certainly have, for such a fine lad. Too bad about his father. I'll speak to Jimmy about a job on the way home."

"Goody!" Flossie said.

"If Jimmy finds his buried pirate treasures," Freddie spoke up, "maybe his grandma won't have to work any more."

Mr. Bobbsey looked mystified. But the twins had no chance to explain what Freddie meant. All of a sudden, mingled with the noise of the departing train, came frantic barking and shouts from the direction of the baggage area.

"Oh dear!" Nan cried. She saw her twin trying to hold onto Snap, who was pulling wildly at his leash. Jimmy, too, was having a hard time restraining Laddie.

"There's the mean dog, Daddy." Flossie pointed fearfully. The black dog was out of his crate, and a leash dangled from his collar. He growled and bared his teeth at Snap and Laddie.

Mr. Bobbsey frowned. "Where's the dog's owner? He has no right to let his pet roam around loose."

The twins' father started forward to help the two boys. Just then Snap gave a tremendous leap forward and twisted away from Bert's grasp. The black dog turned tail and raced directly toward Flossie.

"Look out!" Freddie warned.

It was too late. The black dog ran smack into the little girl. Flossie fell backward, but Mrs. Bobbsey caught her daughter. Snoop, meanwhile, had jumped from Flossie's arms and streaked up the platform.

The black dog now continued his flight, pursued hotly by Snap. Bert raced after his pet, and Jimmy, still holding the collie, followed close behind.

"Oh!" said Flossie tearfully. "Snap and Snoop will both get lost."

Finally, at the far end of the station house, Bert managed to catch up to Snap. He gripped the dog's leash and ordered:

"You stay with me! No more wild chases!"

Snap, panting, heeded his young master and did not try to run any farther. Jimmy and Laddie stopped, too. The black dog stood a few yards ahead, looking back and whining.

"I guess," said Jimmy breathlessly, "his bark is worse than his bite."

"Yes," Bert agreed. "Our dogs called his bluff."

Just then the boys were startled to hear a voice say harshly:

"Rags! You come here, or I'll whip you!"

The black dog put his tail between his legs and slunk past Bert and Jimmy. They turned to see who had spoken. Bert stifled a cry of surprise.

The owner of the mean dog was the man with the scar on his cheek!

The man grabbed the animal's leash. He threw the boys a piercing glance, then hastened away, yanking Rags roughly along.

"Whew!" Jimmy exclaimed. "No wonder the dog is unfriendly, with that kind of treatment."

Bert told Jimmy how Rags's owner had seemed to be listening intently to the story of the buried treasure.

"That's funny," said Jimmy. "I never saw the man before."

The boys rejoined the others, to find them looking at the station roof in consternation.

"Snoop climbed up there after he ran away," Freddie said. "And he won't come down."

"It's that mean old dog's fault," Flossie wailed.

The Bobbsey cat was crouched atop the roof, waving his tail indignantly. He certainly showed no signs of leaving his perch!

Everyone took turns coaxing the cat to descend. But it was no use. Snoop did not budge.

Finally Jimmy proposed a plan. "I can shin up one of those pillars to the roof," he said. "I've had lots of practice climbing apple trees."

Before anyone could stop him, Jimmy started scrambling up the pillar. He used his arms and legs as nimbly as a monkey. The Bobbseys and Dinah watched tensely.

At last Jimmy reached the overhang and swung himself onto the sloping roof.

"Do be careful," Mrs. Bobbsey called.

Inch by inch Jimmy pulled himself up toward the peak of the roof. Snoop watched the boy's approach warily. Now Jimmy spoke softly to the cat:

"Nice Snoop. I'm going to help you get down. Don't be afraid."

The Bobbseys held their breath. Would Jimmy succeed in rescuing their pet?

CHAPTER III

WALK THE PLANK!

AFTER a suspenseful few moments, Snoop slowly came down the roof toward Jimmy.

"I'm so glad!" murmured Nan, and her family heaved relieved sighs.

Jimmy reached out one arm and gently took hold of Snoop. The cat did not try to get away, and the boy cautiously felt his way toward the edge of the station roof.

From below Bert called, "I'll catch Snoop. Can you hang on, Jim?"

"I'm okay. Here comes Snoop!"

Flossie and Freddie were holding Snap's and Laddie's leashes. The small twins hardly dared look.

"I wish Snoop had a parachute," said Freddie fearfully.

The next second the Bobbsey cat came streaking through the air and landed squarely on Bert's shoulder.

"He's safe! He's safe!" Flossie cried joyously, as she lifted the pet into her own arms.

"Thanks to Jimmy's fine rescue," added Mr. Bobbsey, smiling.

Jimmy slid down the pillar to the ground. The family and Dinah Johnson were loud in their praise. He blushed and said modestly:

"Glad I could help my new friends."

Upon learning that Jimmy's grandmother could not meet him, the twins' father offered to drive him home.

"Thank you, sir."

The little procession started from the platform toward the Bobbsey station wagon. Nan had taken Laddie's leash, since Jimmy was carrying one of the Bobbseys' suitcases as well as his own.

Suddenly the collie gave a yelp of pain and jumped into the air. Nan whirled about. Instantly she saw what had happened. A sullen-looking boy about Bert's age, but larger, had pulled Laddie's tail hard.

"Danny Rugg!" Nan cried. "How can you be so mean!"

Danny was a bully who frequently made trouble for the twins and their friends. Now the unpleasant boy retreated a few steps, but sneered:

"Who's that big show-off? The one that got your dumb cat off the roof?"

"He's not a show-off," retorted Flossie indignantly. "Jimmy Dodge is a very brave boy. He's just come to live in Lakeport."

"Yes," Freddie spoke up. "He helps animals instead of hurting them."

"Yah, yah—isn't that sweet!" jeered Danny. "Well, if he comes around our neighborhood, I'll show him who's brave."

"We'll see about that," declared Bert angrily as his twin patted Laddie's head soothingly.

In the meantime Mr. and Mrs. Bobbsey and Dinah had reached the family car. "Children!" called Mrs. Bobbsey. "Hurry!"

Turning their backs on Danny, the twins and Jimmy went to join the grownups. "Don't mind Danny," Bert said to Jimmy. "If he ever makes trouble for you, just let me know!"

Jimmy grinned. "I will."

Suitcases were quickly stowed in the rear compartment of the station wagon, and everyone climbed in. Bert and Jimmy took places in the back, with the two dogs. Nan, in the front seat with her parents, held Snoop. The black cat was fast asleep.

From the driver's seat Mr. Bobbsey asked, "What street do you live on, Jimmy?"

"Glenwood Place. Grandma told me what the house looks like, so I'll know when we get there."

Bert and Nan said nothing, but they knew this was in a poor section of town. As if reading their thoughts, Jimmy added, "Grandma says it's not

—not so nice as where we were in Belleville. But she'll make it seem like home anyway."

"She must be a wonderful person," said Mrs. Bobbsey warmly. "Please bring her to call on us, Jimmy."

"Oh, she'd love that," replied the boy enthusiastically.

"I understand, Jimmy," Mr. Bobbsey said, "you'd like a job before school opens. Would you be interested in helping out at my lumberyard afternoons?"

"Would I?" Jimmy burst out. "Yes, sir! Thanks a million!"

"Good. If you can start day after tomorrow, Monday, I'll help you obtain working papers first thing that morning," said the twins' father. "Then you can report to my office in the afternoon at two."

"I'll be there." Jimmy looked happier than the twins had seen him. "At least I'll have some good news for my grandmother. Won't we, Laddie?" He gave his dog a pat.

Nan thought—if only they could help Jimmy find some clue to his father's whereabouts! "I have a feeling Captain Dodge is still alive," she told herself.

As they drove in the direction of Glenwood Place, Freddie spoke up wistfully, "If Jimmy's going to be at the lumberyard, how can we look for the pirate maps and find the treasure?"

"Oh, we'll look mornings," Flossie said promptly. "We'll just have to get up real early."

The children then took turns telling Mr. Bobbsey and Dinah about Captain Dodge's having buried the iron boxes on different islands.

"Jimmy was blindfolded so he couldn't see where they were hidden," Freddie explained.

"And we have to find the pirate charts to know where to hunt," Flossie added.

"Sakes alive!" Dinah exclaimed. "Looks like you twins got yourselves into a real pirate mystery!"

Freddie remembered something. "Daddy," he said, "can't you build us a big boat so we can all go look for Jimmy's treasure?"

Mr. Bobbsey chuckled as he left the main part of town. "That's a tall order," he said. "But maybe I can supply a smaller boat for you to search the local islands."

"You mean the lumberyard launch?" guessed Nan.

"Yes."

"Super, Dad!" Bert cried.

"It sure would be," Jimmy agreed. "If I only had the charts my father drew!"

"Perhaps they will turn up," Mrs. Bobbsey remarked. "Papers can easily be mislaid in the process of moving."

"I'll look through everything again," Jimmy said.

Freddie suddenly turned to Flossie, who sat between him and Dinah. "I'm a pirate chief, and you're my prisoner. Walk the plank!"

Flossie giggled. Without warning, the little girl stood up on the seat. "All right, pirate Freddie. Here I go—oh!"

The prisoner lost her balance and tumbled sideways into Dinah's lap. "Oof!" exclaimed the startled cook. "You all better not be pirates till we get home."

"Freddie and Flossie," their mother reprimanded, "please sit still while we're driving."

The small twins settled back in their seats, and Flossie said with a giggle, "Thanks, Dinah, for saving me from jumping off the plank."

Mr. Bobbsey now turned down the street where Jimmy lived. The lad pointed to a green house halfway down the block. "My grandmother and I live there."

Nan and her mother gazed at the shabby dwellings and unkempt yards of the neighborhood. It all looked very uninviting.

Mr. Bobbsey parked the station wagon in front of the green house. "Well, Jimmy, I'll see you Monday morning," he said smilingly.

"I'll be ready," Jimmy promised.

Bert held Laddie until his new friend had climbed out with his suitcase. Then Jimmy took his collie's leash.

"Good-by," he said. "Thanks a lot for everything."

"Good-by! Good-by!" chorused the twins and their parents, and Dinah called out the window, "When you come see us, I'll bake a real special cake with fudge icing."

Jimmy grinned. "That's my favorite kind, Dinah!"

Bert went up to the front steps with him. "So long, Jimmy. Let us know if ou find those charts."

"I will. So long."

As Bert went back toward the station wagon, he glanced up the street. In the gathering twilight he spotted a taxi parked in front of a house three doors away from Jimmy's. The car's engine was running. There was just enough light for the boy to see the lone passenger.

In the back seat, staring at the green house, was the scar-faced man!

CHAPTER IV

OVERBOARD!

BERT hopped into the station wagon. "Dad!" he said excitedly. "I think that taxi parked up the street followed us here on purpose."

Quickly he told his family about the scar-faced man and his interest in Jimmy's story.

"So," Bert went on, "he must have been waiting near the station till he saw Jimmy leave with us. Then he started trailing our car."

Mrs. Bobbsey looked worried. "I hope he's not going to make trouble for the Dodges."

"Jimmy said he never saw the man before," Bert told her.

Flossie looked back at the taxi, which still stood at the curb. "Oo!" she shuddered. "He looks like a real bad pirate.

At the same instant the stranger in the cab looked directly at the Bobbseys. When he saw Flossie and the others staring at him, he leaned forward and spoke to the driver. With a roar, the taxi started up, sped down the street past the station wagon, and disappeared around the corner.

"He sure acts suspicious," Bert stated.

"Yes," Nan agreed. She turned to her father. "We'd better warn Jimmy to be on the lookout, don't you think, Dad?"

"Yes, I do," said Mr. Bobbsey. "And if Mrs. Dodge sees that man around, she should report it to the police."

It was almost dark by the time Mr. Bobbsey pulled into the driveway of their large, rambling home. Quickly the bags were taken out, and everyone went inside. Dinah had hustled into the kitchen with Mrs. Bobbsey.

Soon a late supper of cold chicken, potato salad, and hot biscuits was ready. Everyone ate hungrily.

The twins slept soundly that night after their day's trip and excitement. Freddie, however, dreamed he was on an island all by himself digging for pirate gold.

"And did you find any?" Flossie asked him the next morning when her twin told of his dream while they were playing.

"No," Freddie complained. "I didn't have any maps."

The family went to church and spent the day quietly. Monday morning Mr. Bobbsey set out early to assist Jimmy in getting his working papers. A little later he telephoned the twins to say that everything was in order for their new friend to begin his job.

Soon after lunch Flossie and Freddie went into the side yard. Suddenly they heard two voices.

"Hi, Freddie!"

"Hello, Floss!"

Two of the small twins' friends came running up. One was Johnnie Wilson, Freddie's playmate. The other was Alice Boyd. She and Flossie often "played house" together with their dolls.

The two little girls decided they would play this game now. "I'll get Linda," said Flossie, referring to her favorite doll.

Freddie, meanwhile, drew Johnnie aside. "Let's go down to the lake by the lumberyard," he said, "and practice looking for Jimmy's buried treasure."

"Who's Jimmy? What treasure?" Johnnie asked curiously.

Freddie quickly told him the story of Jimmy Dodge, his missing father, and the buried treasures.

Johnnie's eyes grew wide. "Oh boy!" he cried. "I want to help Jimmy hunt, too."

Mrs. Bobbsey came outside just then to pick some flowers from the garden. The boys ran over and told her their plan.

"All right," she said. "Be sure to let your father know that you're going to play near the lake, Freddie."

The little boy promised to do this. He raced inside the house and was back in a minute carrying two toy sailboats.

"We'll need these to carry the treasure," Freddie said as he and Johnnie, with Snap, set off toward Mr. Bobbsey's lumberyard.

Nan and Bert, too, had left for their father's office to see Jimmy. When they reached it, they found that the boy had arrived early. Mr. Bobbsey was introducing Jimmy to Sam Johnson.

Sam was as jolly as his wife Dinah, but he was thin and wiry. Now he flashed his wide smile at Jimmy.

"Real pleased to know you," said Sam. "And we can sure use your help here. We're mighty busy now."

Nan and Bert had entered the room and quietly found chairs. Jimmy's face lit up when he saw the twins.

"Hi!" he greeted them. "You know, when Grandma saw Laddie, and then I told her about meeting you Bobbseys, and coming to work here, she looked almost cheerful, the way she used to before my father was lost."

"I'm glad," said Nan, touched. "Bert and I came to tell you we saw that man with the scar on his face near your house Saturday night."

When she and Bert had finished their story, Jimmy shook his head. "I can't figure out what he wants. I did tell my grandmother about him. But she never saw anybody like him, either."

"Well," Mr. Bobbsey said, "we'll all keep on the watch for the fellow, whoever he is."

At this moment, Freddie and Johnnie, followed by Snap, came bursting into the office. Each boy was clutching a sailboat.

"Jimmy," Freddie said, "is it all right if Johnnie Wilson and I pretend we're looking for your treasures?"

Jimmy grinned. "Sure. If you find them, watch out for pirates!"

Everybody laughed. Sam had been listening to the conversation with a puzzled expression. Bert now told him what it was all about.

"Well," said Sam wisely, "the twins here are pretty good at finding lost things."

In the past the four children had solved some mysteries, both at home and on trips.

"Jimmy," Nan said thoughtfully, "do you know the name of the island your father buried the first treasure on?"

The boy shook his head. "That's the trouble. I can't remember the one we went to on my seventh birthday, except it isn't too far from here." Jimmy added that he could recall the others. "But of course I can't look on those islands till I'm the right age."

Jimmy glanced at the clock on the wall. "It's after two," he said to Mr. Bobbsey. "Time for me to go to work."

The twins' father smiled. "You're very conscientious. You can go with Sam. He'll show you what jobs you're to take care of."

Sam and Jimmy said good-by and hurried off. Nan and Bert left, too. They had promised their mother to do some shopping for her on their way home.

"We're going down to the dock now," Freddie told his father.

"All right. Let Mike know where you'll be. And stay where it's shallow."

Mike Donovan was the good-natured, capable day watchman at the lumberyard. The two little boys, with Snap at their heels, ran through the bustling, noisy mill yard. Reaching the Lake Metoka dock, they saw Mike coming toward them.

"Well, Freddie and Johnnie," said the husky watchman, "going to do a bit o' sailing today?"

"Yes—across the ocean to find pirate treasure," declared Freddie. He stooped at the edge of the dock and lowered his sailboat. Johnnie did the same.

The boys stood up, letting out the strings attached to their craft. The toy sails billowed as the boats went scudding along in the brisk breeze.

"Sight any treasure yet?" called Mike with a grin.

The playmates shaded their eyes and squinted, as if scanning the horizon.

"Not yet, Mike," Freddie reported. Suddenly he had another idea. He would put some treasure aboard his boat. What could he use?

"I know!" Freddie thought. "I have ten brand-new pennies." He had been saving them to put into his piggy bank.

He dug into the pocket of his jeans and brought out the pennies. Clutching them in one hand, he pulled in his boat with the other.

Freddie began dropping his pennies inside the sailboat. A sudden gust of wind sent the boat scudding away. The little craft tipped far over on one side.

"Hey!" Freddie shouted. "My treasure's overboard!"

He watched in dismay as the seven pennies spilled out of the sailboat and sank.

"How're you going to get them back?" Johnnie asked, staring at the water. It was shallow enough so that the boys could see the shiny coppers lying on the sandy bottom.

Freddie put the other three pennies back into his pocket and looked around. Mike was talking to one of the mill workers.

"I think I can wade in," Freddie told his friend. "You stay here so I'll know where to look."

He handed the strings of his boat to Johnnie. Then Freddie rolled up his jeans and took off his socks and sneakers.

Freddie waded out until he was almost opposite Johnny. The water was deeper than he had thought. His jeans, though rolled up above his knees, were already wet.

"If you go out much farther you'll be in swimming," Johnny called to him.

Freddie did not know what to do. His pennies were only a few steps away. How could he reach them without getting thoroughly soaked?

At this point Snap began running back and forth along the dock. He barked loudly, as if to warn his young master.

"Freddie Bobbsey!" someone shouted. "You'd better get in here quick!"

The little boy turned around to see Mike standing on the shore. The watchman had a stern look on his face. Sadly Freddie waded back. He had lost his pennies for good, and now he knew he would be scolded for going into the water without permission.

"I'm sorry, Mike," Freddie said when he came up to the man. "I—I was just trying to rescue my treasure." He explained what had happened.

Johnnie had come off the dock and was holding the boats. "Will Freddie's pennies have to stay under the lake forever?" he asked.

Mike's expression had softened. He looked straight at Freddie. "You promise never to go in the water here unless you tell me?"

Freddie nodded vigorously. Then, to his delight, Mike himself waded out and retrieved all of Freddie's pennies.

"Next time we'll look for the treasure on land," the small twin declared as he and Johnnie and Snap started for home.

Meanwhile Nan and Bert, who had finished shopping for their mother, were on the way home. Carrying several parcels, the older twins turned the corner toward their house.

Suddenly a piercing scream came from the direction of the Bobbseys' side porch.

"That's Flossie!" Nan gasped.

CHAPTER V

THE YOUNG SPY

BERT and Nan raced up onto the side porch and flung their parcels on a table. Flossie was crying, and Alice Boyd looked frightened.

"What's the matter?" Nan asked, putting her arms around her small sister.

Flossie choked back a sob. "Th—that awful black dog ran right up here and grabbed my doll Linda right out of her crib!"

Nan gasped and Bert cried, "You mean the black dog called Rags that belongs to the scarfaced man?"

Flossie nodded vigorously. "And Rags was growling just the way he did on the train."

Alice gave a little shiver. "You mean that bad dog is following you Bobbseys?" she wanted to know.

Bert and Nan shook their heads. Each had the same thought. Was the owner of the black dog in their vicinity? And why? First he had seemed to be spying on the Dodges' place, and now the Bobbsey home.

Not wishing to alarm the little girls any further, Bert said calmly, "I'll find your doll, Flossie. Which way did the dog go?"

"Over there." She pointed to the rear of the yard, which was bordered by a high hedge. Bert dashed in that direction.

Reaching the hedge, he heard hissing and growling sounds coming from the other side. Dropping to his knees, Bert peered through an opening in the hedge to the driveway behind it.

"Snoop!" he exclaimed in surprise.

The Bobbsey pet stood on the drive. His back arched, Snoop's green eyes blazed, and his bristling tail switched back and forth angrily.

"P—ss-sst!" hissed the cat.

The cause of Snoop's fury was the black dog Rags! He crouched about five feet away, uttering low growls. Halfway between the two animals lay Flossie's doll.

Bert had to smile. "Good for Snoop," he thought. "He's getting even with Rags."

By this time Nan, Flossie, and Alice had run up to see what was happening. Bert put a finger to his lips and beckoned them to peek through the hedge. At the sight of Snoop holding the unfriendly dog at bay, the three girls laughed.

"How are you going to get Linda?" Flossie asked, looking worried again.

For answer, Bert lay down flat on his stomach and began to inch his way forward. The hole in the hedge was just large enough for him to squeeze through. Bert stretched out his hand for the doll and grasped her arm.

All this time Snoop and Rags kept glaring at each other. Bert pulled Linda slowly toward him. The dog's eyes were attracted by the moving doll. Without hesitation, Snoop gave a piercing *me-ow!* and charged at the intruder.

This was too much for Rags. With a terrified yelp, he turned and raced down the driveway to the sidewalk.

Hastily Bert backed through the hedge and handed Flossie her doll. "Quick, Nan," he said. "Let's see where Rags goes!"

Warning the smaller girls to remain in the yard, brother and sister dashed to the front of their house.

"Look!" Nan pointed up the street.

On the corner a short distance away, Bert and Nan saw Rags. The black dog was being yanked along roughly by a man who wore his hat pulled low.

"It's Mr. Scarface, all right," Bert declared. "I recognize his voice."

The stranger was scolding the animal harshly in loud tones. The twins heard him say, "Stupid! Why did you have to go in there? You'll spoil everything—"

The rest of the man's words trailed off as he proceeded farther along the street.

"Oh, Bert!" Nan cried. "What does he mean? 'Spoil' what?"

"Search me," her twin replied. "But let's shadow him and try to find out."

Bert and Nan started off. They decided to keep a block between themselves and the scar-faced man. Every time he slowed his pace or looked over his shoulder, the children dodged in back of the nearest tree or shrub.

"Do you suppose he lives in Lakeport?" Nan whispered to Bert presently as they stepped from behind a large hydrangea bush.

"I'll bet he does now—or is staying some place not far from town," her brother replied.

Just then Bert saw one of his best friends, Charlie Mason, crossing the street toward them.

"Hi, Bert and Nan!" Charlie called. "What're you doing—playing tree-tag?"

The good-looking boy, who was twelve, joined the twins. "Hi!" Bert and Nan said in whispers. Before they could explain further, the strange man ahead stopped abruptly and turned completely around.

"Behind this tree, quick!" Bert urged.

The three darted in back of a large oak. But it was too late. The scar-faced man had evidently recognized the Bobbseys, for he broke into a run, dragging his dog with him.

The twins gave chase, followed by the puzzled Charlie. The man rounded the corner at the next street, and when the children reached the spot there was no one in sight.

"Oh-oh!" Bert muttered. He pointed to a taxi going off in the distance. In a moment it turned into another road.

The twins heaved sighs of disappointment, and Nan said, "That man must have told the taxi driver to wait for him here." Bert agreed.

Charlie looked more mystified than ever.

"What's this all about anyway?" he demanded. "You two act like detectives."

"Here's the story," said Bert.

He explained as the trio started back toward the Bobbsey house. By the time they reached it, Charlie knew about Jimmy Dodge, his hidden treasures, and the mysterious stranger.

"Nan and I think," Bert went on as they strolled up the front walk, "that Mr. Scarface is spying on the Dodges—and on our house, too."

"Whizzikers!" Charlie whistled. "You sure brought a bunch of mysteries back with you!"

At this point Flossie and Freddie came running from the house to meet them. The small twins had just exchanged stories about their afternoon's adventures. Alice and Johnnie had gone home.

"Did you catch the bad man?" Flossie asked Nan and Bert anxiously.

Nan shook her head. "No. We think he and his dog rode away in a taxi, so we couldn't follow."

Freddie felt disappointed that he had not been home during the excitement. "Snap and I would have chased him in my fire engine," he declared stoutly.

The twins and Charlie sat down under a maple tree on the side lawn. The late afternoon sun was very hot, and everyone was thirsty. Nan went into the house and returned with a tray of lemonade and freshly baked spice cookies. As the children ate, their talk turned once more to Jimmy Dodge and his island treasures.

Nan said, "If only Jimmy could remember some of the directions on his first chart!"

"Or," Flossie put in, "which island he went to on his seventh birthday."

Just then Nan's eyes were drawn to the evergreen shrubbery at the corner of the house. She saw that the branches were moving.

"Someone's hiding behind those bushes," she told the others in a low tone.

Everyone stared at the shrubs. The branches moved again. Bert sprang to his feet.

"Come out, whoever you are!" he ordered.

"Oh, I hope it's not that pirate man," Flossie said fearfully.

Bert advanced slowly toward the evergreens. Suddenly from the far side, a familiar figure dashed out and ran across the lawn.

"Danny Rugg!" Bert exclaimed. "Why were you spying on us?"

"Try and find out!" Danny called as he raced off.

"Okay, I will," said Bert and raced after the bully. Charlie had jumped to his feet and joined the chase.

The girls and Freddie rose and looked at one another in dismay.

"Do you think Danny heard everything we said about the treasure?" Freddie asked worriedly.

"I'm afraid so," Nan replied. "I hope he won't try to hunt for it."

By now Bert and Charlie had overtaken Danny.

"Why were you hiding in our bushes and how long were you there?" Bert demanded.

Danny guffawed. "Wouldn't you like to know?" he jeered. "You Bobbseys think you're so smart. Huh! I'll bet I can find that treasure Jimmy's bragging about."

Bert retorted angrily, *"You'll* be smart if you mind your own business, Danny!"

"Maybe we'd better teach him how," added Charlie, doubling up his fists.

Danny backed away. "All right, all right," he whined. "No fair two against one. Besides, I don't believe Jimmy really has any old buried treasure."

Bert and Charlie did not bother to answer the unpleasant boy. In disgust, they turned and hurried back to the house. "Next time Danny won't get off so easy," Bert declared as the boys opened the screen door to the side porch.

They found the girls and Freddie talking with Mrs. Bobbsey. She looked concerned and said to Bert, "Nan has just told me about that man and his dog being near here. Your father must notify the police as soon as he comes home."

The children agreed, but secretly Bert hoped

that he could dig up some clues about the mysterious stranger himself.

"Here come Daddy and Sam!" cried Freddie, seeing Mr. Bobbsey's car turn into the drive.

"And Jimmy's with them!" Flossie exclaimed.

The twins, followed by Charlie, ran to meet their father and the others.

Sam grinned broadly. "Jimmy sure was a mighty big help at the yard today," he told them.

Mr. Bobbsey placed a hand on the lad's shoulder, and said warmly, "He's an excellent worker."

Jimmy's face glowed at the praise. "Thank you," he said simply.

The twins then introduced Charlie to their new friend. Charlie asked, "Okay if I go along on your island treasure hunt?"

"You bet," Jimmy replied with a grin.

A little later Charlie said good-by and went home to supper. The twins were delighted to learn that Jimmy was to stay overnight at the Bobbsey home. Mrs. Bobbsey had telephoned his grandmother to invite both the Dodges to have dinner with them.

"But Mrs. Dodge has to work this evening," she added, "and won't be able to join us."

Jimmy spoke up a little shyly, "Grandma wants to meet the twins very much, Mrs. Bobbsey. Could they come to our house to lunch tomorrow?"

"Oh, that will be nice." Nan turned to her mother. "May we, please?"

"Why, certainly," Mrs. Bobbsey smiled, touched by the invitation. She knew it was not easy for the Dodges to have much company at present.

"Goody!" Flossie exclaimed. "We can look for the treasure maps!"

All the children accepted this idea with enthusiasm. "After supper," Bert said to Jimmy, "could you show us what pirate maps look like?"

"Sure. I can remember some of the marks on the ones my father drew."

Suddenly Nan's face clouded. "Dad," she said, "we're worried about something."

"Yes?"

She related the chase after the scar-faced man. When Nan had finished, Mr. Bobbsey looked grave and said, "I'll call headquarters right away. Bert and Jimmy, you can tell Chief Smith some details about the fellow, too."

By the time the three had given a full report to the Lakeport police officer, supper was ready. Everyone sat down at the table and Dinah served one of the family's favorite dishes, roast beef and browned potatoes. During the meal Bert told the others that Police Chief Smith had promised to alert his men about the suspicious stranger.

Jimmy had become rather quiet and had

eaten little. Flossie noticed this and asked him, "Don't you feel well?"

Jimmy put down his fork and burst out, "I'm afraid that man, whoever he is, will make trouble for you Bobbseys, and all because of me."

The twins and their parents begged Jimmy not to worry on their account, and Mr. Bobbsey reassured him with a big smile. "We're used to mysteries in this household!"

"That's a fact." Dinah chuckled as she carried in a luscious cake. "Now, Jimmy," she coaxed, "you just try a big piece of this. It's got fudge icing."

Jimmy had brightened considerably. "I'd love some, Dinah," he said.

As soon as supper was over, Mr. and Mrs. Bobbsey said they must leave to attend a charity group meeting.

"If you hear or see anything suspicious," Mr. Bobbsey told the older twins, "be sure to let Sam know. He'll be here all evening."

"We will, Dad," Bert promised.

The children went into the living room. Flossie and Freddie pulled up chairs around a small table, and they all sat down. Nan gave paper and pencil to Jimmy.

Eagerly the twins looked on as he sketched rapidly. After a minute he held up the sheet of paper for inspection.

"This will give you an idea about the maps of

the old pirates," said Jimmy. "Most of the men those days couldn't read or write, so they used simple marks like these." He pointed to several on his sketch. "This X would stand for the place where the treasure was buried. The T might mean a tree, and the circle could be a rock or a hill."

Bert nodded, then asked, "What do you think the numbers on your father's charts meant?"

Jimmy thought deeply for a moment. Finally he replied, "I'm pretty sure Dad used the numbers for a code telling the name of the island and directions for finding the spot where the treasure's buried. But I can't remember the numbers."

"Well," Freddie spoke up hopefully, "we'll hunt real hard for the maps tomorrow."

Suddenly Snap, who had been dozing beneath the open window, gave a growl. He sprang up and put his paws on the sill, barking excitedly.

The twins and Jimmy exchanged glances. They had heard no sound of footsteps. Had someone crept up noiselessly through the dusk to peer into the house? Mr. Scarface, perhaps?

CHAPTER VI

THE ATTIC SEARCH

BERT and Jimmy dashed to the front door and flung it open. They peered into the gathering darkness as Snap raced outside.

"I don't see anybody," Bert whispered.

"I don't either," said Jimmy.

Sam, followed by Dinah, came hurrying from the kitchen. "What's botherin' old Snap?" Sam asked.

"He heard something—or somebody—outside," Bert answered. "Let's see what Snap found. I don't hear him barking now."

Sam and the boys cautiously went out, as Dinah warned, "You all be careful." She and the girls watched anxiously from the doorway and Freddie stood on the front step.

The searchers, meanwhile, started looking about the Bobbsey property. They noticed nothing unusual and did not see or hear Snap.

"I'll bet that dog is just playin' hide-and-seek with us," Sam said finally.

Bert shook his head, puzzled. "Snap never barks like that unless he's surprised by something."

The three continued on around the house. All of a sudden they stopped and stared in astonishment. In the rear yard Snap and another dog were chasing each other in circles.

"Why, it's Laddie!" shouted Jimmy.

"So your collie is the mysterious visitor." Bert laughed. "Snap recognized him."

The two pets came bounding over, and Jimmy patted the collie. "Poor Laddie. Guess you must've got lonesome without me and Grandma at home." He explained that the puppy usually did not wander off.

"Well," Sam chuckled, "he might as well stay here overnight, too."

Later Jimmy telephoned his grandmother, who by then had returned home from work. Mrs. Dodge said Laddie must have jumped out a window which had been left open.

"Land sakes," declared Dinah. "We've had 'nough jitters for one day."

Freddie nodded solemnly. "But not enough cookies. Are there any left, Dinah?"

"Just enough to go around—and I'll make some nice fruit drink, too."

The children enjoyed a late snack, and Flossie

gave Snap and Laddie several dog biscuits. At bedtime, the children went upstairs. Jimmy would share Bert and Freddie's room, where there was an extra cot. Nan and Flossie said good night to them and went to their own room.

"See you pirates at breakfast," Nan giggled.

The twins and their guest rose early the next morning. Dinah had prepared a tasty breakfast of waffles and bacon, and soon the family and Jimmy appeared. When Mr. and Mrs. Bobbsey heard of Laddie's unexpected arrival the previous evening, they laughed.

"I'm glad he didn't get lost looking for you, Jimmy," said Mr. Bobbsey.

The visitor smiled. "I guess Laddie got used to finding me when we were at the farm."

Mr. Bobbsey left for the lumberyard saying he would see Jimmy at work that afternoon. "Good luck in your search for the charts," he added.

Mrs. Bobbsey offered to drive the children to the Dodges. Before setting off, Bert phoned police headquarters.

"No, Bert," Chief Smith replied to the boy's query, "we haven't spotted that scar-faced man. He must be lying low for the present. Call me right away if you see him again."

Everyone climbed into the station wagon. All the way to Jimmy's house the twins and their friend kept on the lookout for the mysterious stranger or his dog. But nobody saw the pair.

"Maybe he got scared when you chased him yesterday," Freddie said to Nan and Bert.

The older twins doubted this. The man seemed very persistent. "Whatever his scheme is, I don't think he'll give it up so easily," said Bert.

"But I can't see," said Jimmy, "why he'd risk stealing my five treasures that Dad buried around here." He explained that while his father had not told him what was in the hidden boxes, the Captain had hinted that the contents were not of tremendous value.

Bert snapped his fingers. "But what about the last treasure your father hid on the Pacific island? Maybe Scarface is trying to find out where it is. He must've heard somebody say that one's valuable."

Jimmy's eyes opened wide. "Maybe you're right! Oh, do you suppose I'll ever be able to look for it there?"

Soon Mrs. Bobbsey pulled up in front of the house where the Dodges lived. Everyone got out and followed Jimmy inside and upstairs to the second floor. Laddie frisked on ahead.

At the end of a short hallway a door opened. A frail, sweet-looking woman came out.

"Grandma," Jimmy said, giving her a hug, "here are the Bobbseys."

Mrs. Dodge gave them a warm smile. "I'm so

glad to meet Jimmy's new friends. Please come in."

"Thank you." Mrs. Bobbsey smiled back as she and the twins entered the apartment. Although plainly furnished, the rooms were brightened by gay curtains and colorful hooked rugs.

"Did you make the rugs, Mrs. Dodge?" Nan asked admiringly.

The elderly woman nodded. "Yes. They're one of the few reminders I've kept of—of happier days."

For a second her eyes glistened with tears, then she went on more cheerfully, "But thanks to you Bobbseys, and all you've done for Jimmy, we both feel at home in Lakeport already."

"Jimmy's done a lot for us," Flossie spoke up as they sat down in the living room. "And he's going to let us hunt for the pirate maps and his birthday treasure."

"That's fine," said Mrs. Dodge. "My son would be delighted, I know, to have you twins help in the search." She smiled a little. "The island pirate game was a secret between Jimmy and his father. So of course I don't know where the treasures are hidden."

She explained that the last time she had seen the charts was before the move from Belleville. "Being still so upset over my son's disappearance," Mrs. Dodge went on, "I might have misplaced them while packing. But I'm sure the

maps were in a Manila envelope which was with
the items put into the moving van."

"Maybe," Nan said, "the movers didn't notice
it, and the maps were left behind."

Jimmy suggested telephoning the Dodges' former landlady in Belleville to ask about this.

"I should have thought of that," Mrs. Dodge
said, adding that Mrs. Wheeler, the landlady,
had assisted her with the packing and other moving day chores.

Jimmy hurried to the telephone, while the
Bobbseys chatted with their hostess. Freddie's
eyes, meanwhile, wandered about the room. He
had noticed several objects connected with the
sea. A picture of Captain Dodge's *Flying Dolphin* hung on one wall.

Below the picture stood a small open cabinet,
inside of which was the model of an old-time
sailing ship's anchor.

Freddie's gaze stopped at the miniature of a
ship on a nearby table.

"Oh," he thought, "I'd like to sail in a boat like
that!"

Fascinated, the little boy slid out of his chair
and went over to the model. He fingered the tiny
masts and rigging. Impulsively he lifted the ves-
sel to look at it more closely. To his horror, the
bow and stern of the model separated in his
hands!

"Oh!" he cried in dismay. "I—I've broken it!"

The other Bobbseys gasped when they realized what had happened.

"Freddie," Mrs. Bobbsey said, frowning, "you know you should not touch anything so fragile."

To her surprise, both the Dodges were smil-

ing. Jimmy had just returned from telephoning. He explained, "Freddie didn't hurt the model at all. It is supposed to come apart. An old sailor made it for my father. The two sections are joined by pegs instead of glue."

Vastly relieved, Freddie put the halves of the model together and placed it on the table.

"Is it the model of an old galleon?" Bert asked Jimmy. "The kind your father said used to carry gold and be waylaid by the pirates?"

"That's right. Galleons were used a lot by European countries in the sixteenth century."

Jimmy then reported that he had tried Mrs. Wheeler's phone number several times, but there had been no answer.

"We'd better start on our map search anyhow," Bert urged.

"I'll pick you up after lunch," the twins' mother told them. "We'll drop Jimmy off at the lumberyard."

She offered to drive Mrs. Dodge to the dress shop. "That's very kind of you," Jimmy's grandmother said. "But the shop is close by, and I won't mind the walk."

Good-bys were exchanged, and both Dodges thanked Mrs. Bobbsey for the family's hospitality to Jimmy.

"We loved having him," she said to the boy's grandmother. "Next time we want you to come, too."

"And Dinah will fix an extra good supper," Flossie declared.

"That will be wonderful," Mrs. Dodge said, and Jimmy grinned.

Five minutes later, the children, accompanied

by Laddie, were ascending the steps to the storage attic, on the top floor of the house. Jimmy had obtained the key from his grandmother and now unlocked the door.

The searchers crowded into the rather musty room. It had only one small window, through which the light dimly filtered. Jimmy turned on the single light, and everyone looked about.

"Where shall we start?" Freddie asked.

Jimmy indicated an assortment of cartons, trunks, and pieces of household equipment in one corner. "Those are the things Grandma brought from Belleville."

He and the twins decided that each one would hunt in a different box or trunk. For a while the children were silent as they carefully lifted out various items: photographs, bundles of letters, paintings, and books. Laddie ran from one spot to another, sniffing curiously.

Flossie sighed as she finished emptying a carton. "Oh dear. The maps aren't here."

The others had no luck either. At last only one large upright wardrobe trunk remained to be searched. It was not locked, but was so heavy the three boys had difficulty in pulling it open.

Finally the big trunk was opened wide. The Bobbseys stared in wonder at the contents.

"Wow!" Freddie gave a whoop. "Pirate outfits —and a sword, too!"

Sure enough, on the trunk's rack hung brilliant

shirts and breeches. Tucked among them in a sheath was a curved blade with a carved handle.

Nan looked at Jimmy. "Are these the costumes you and your father wore to bury the treasures?"

"Yes," the boy replied proudly. "Dad brought his back from the old pirate haunts. Grandma made my costumes."

He took them out one by one and passed them around. Nan held up a small green shirt with red stripes around it and a pair of matching pants.

"You must have worn this on your first island trip," she guessed. "It's a small size."

"You're right." Jimmy laughed. "I even carried a sword. But mine was a wooden copy my father made of this one."

He lifted out the large weapon, and Freddie asked in awe, "Did some pirate use that once?"

"According to the person Dad bought it from, this scimitar belonged to a buccaneer chief," Jimmy answered. His eyes sparkled. "Dad used to wear it with his costumes. He sure looked like the real thing!"

In the drawers of the wardrobe were found different types of pirate headgear. There were red bandannas with dangling gold rings, skull caps, and three-cornered cocked hats.

Bert flourished a tricorn with an immense plume curled around the brim. "This must have belonged to a pirate prince," he said.

"It probably really belonged to a Spanish nobleman, who was called a grandee," Jimmy explained. "The pirates stole not only their gold—but their clothes, too."

Flossie giggled. "Those old pirates must have liked to play dress-up."

For fun Nan took the plumed hat from Bert and set it on her head.

"Huh! Whoever heard of a lady pirate?" Freddie teased.

Suddenly an odd expression came over Nan's face. She lifted the hat slowly from her head and peered into the crown.

"What is it, Nan?" Bert asked curiously.

His sister reached into the tricorn and drew out a crumpled sheet of parchment paper.

"Jimmy," Nan's voice trembled with excitement, "could this be one of your treasure maps?"

CHAPTER VII

WORKING OUT A CODE

THE children crowded around Nan and stared at the wrinkled parchment. On it was a rough sketch and some figures.

"Is it a pirate map, Jimmy?" cried Flossie. "Is it?"

The twins held their breath in suspense as Jimmy took the paper from Nan and studied it closely. A moment later a big smile appeared on his face.

"It seems too good to be true," he said finally, "but this is the map Dad made on my seventh birthday for the first treasure. I can tell because of this number." He pointed to a large *I* on the parchment.

Freddie was so elated he tried to do a handspring. But there was not space enough in the cluttered attic for acrobatics! *Crash!* The little boy almost landed inside the open wardrobe trunk.

"Be careful, Freddie," Flossie giggled. "You'll get packed by mistake."

Her twin picked himself up and went to look at the map, which Jimmy was holding.

"Sure seems like a real pirate chart," Bert remarked.

The drawing consisted of a crudely shaped crescent, with various symbols on it. At the right-hand side was the group of numbers. Flossie bent her curly head close to the map.

"Those are the marks you told us about, Jimmy?" she said, pointing to the symbols. "The T's are for trees, and the circles for rocks?"

Jimmy nodded. "And there's the X," he said. "The place where the treasure's buried!"

"And of course," Nan put in, "the crescent must be the island itself!"

"Can you figure out a way to read the code numbers?" Bert asked Jimmy.

"I hope so. Let's all try it."

The children sat down on the floor, and Jimmy smoothed out the parchment. For a few minutes there was silence as each one puzzled over the list of numbers. Laddie lay down quietly by his master.

"I guess," said Bert at last, "each number really stands for something different."

Jimmy snapped his fingers. "You're right, Bert! That's the key to this code. I remember when Dad started to teach me about deciphering, he said these numbers were used in place of letters."

"So we just have to find which numbers stand for what letters!" Bert rose to his feet. "Let's work it out."

After quickly putting things to rights in the attic, the children trooped downstairs. They found Mrs. Dodge there and told of their discovery. Then Jimmy showed her the treasure map.

"Amazing!" she exclaimed, her face wreathed in smiles. "It's strange, though, how that one became separated from the others."

She went on to say that in the process of packing, it must have slipped out of the envelope. Again Jimmy telephoned to the former landlady, Mrs. Wheeler. This time she was at home, and the twins waited near as he talked with her.

When the conversation was over, he reported with a little smile, "Mrs. Wheeler says she dropped the packet and this map fell out. She thought it was just some old scribbling and stuffed the parchment into the pirate's hat."

"Why?" asked Freddie curiously.

" 'Cause," Flossie piped up, "it's stiff and would help keep the hat from being bent."

"That's exactly the reason," Jimmy said. "Anyhow, Mrs. Wheeler doesn't know what could have happened to the rest of the charts. She thought the movers took the envelope, though."

"Well," Mrs. Dodge remarked, "I'm sure that the twins will help find it."

She then announced that lunch was ready. "You'll have a little time afterward to start figuring out the treasure code."

"Yes," agreed Freddie, "I can think better if I'm not hungry." Everyone laughed.

Jimmy gave Laddie something to eat before sitting down with the others in the small dining room. The meal proved to be simple, but tasty. Freddie finished his serving of dessert, crisp apple cake with cream, and declared, "This is my next favorite to Dinah's fudge cake."

The Bobbsey girls admired the pretty bouquet of marigolds on the table. Mrs. Dodge beamed. "I used to love gardening when Jimmy and his father and I were together," she said. "I have a tiny place in the back yard here where I can plant a few flowers."

When lunch was over, and the dishes washed, the children sat down again at the table. Once more they studied the groups of numbers on the pirate map.

"If we can decipher it," said Nan, "we could start hunting for the treasure tomorrow."

Determinedly Jimmy took paper and pencil and jotted down the first group of numbers in the code. Underneath he placed the corresponding letters of the alphabet. Bert got up from his chair and looked over Jimmy's shoulder.

"Hm," he observed, "it doesn't spell anything if you start from the front of the alphabet."

"That gives me an idea," said Jimmy. "We'll work it backward with Z for one and A for twenty-six."

For several minutes there was silence as the boys wrote. Gradually the letters formed into words.

"Oo—oo!" Flossie squealed, "Horse—shoe—"

"*Island!*" Freddie cried.

"Horseshoe Island!" Nan exclaimed. "Why, I know where that is."

Jimmy looked overjoyed and incredulous all at once. "My first treasure is buried near here?"

The twins nodded excitedly. "Horseshoe's halfway between Lakeport and Belleville." Bert added, "We've never been to that island, but people go there for picnics."

Just then Mrs. Bobbsey arrived to pick up the children. Quickly they took turns telling her of the morning's successful search.

"We still have to uncode the other numbers to get directions to the treasure's hiding place," Jimmy spoke up. "Maybe you twins could work on it this afternoon."

His suggestion was eagerly accepted, and Nan turned to her mother. "Do you think Dad would lend us the lumberyard boat to go to Horseshoe Island tomorrow?"

Mrs. Bobbsey replied, "I'm sure he will, dear. Why don't you ask him about it this afternoon?"

Freddie was so excited at the prospect he grabbed his twin and spun her around. "We're going on a pirate hunt!" he chanted again and again.

The little boy broke off suddenly. "I think we should look like pirates," he burst out. "Jimmy, could we wear your costumes?"

The others thought this would be fun. "Only,"
Bert said, "won't they be too small now?"

Mrs. Dodge immediately offered to make the
necessary alterations. "I can easily let out a few
seams and have the outfits ready by tomorrow
morning," she promised.

Flossie ran to give her a big hug. "Oh, that's
scrumptious!"

Jimmy's grandmother smiled. "I'll enjoy having a little part in the treasure hunt," she said.

A short while later, Mrs. Bobbsey let her children and Jimmy off at the lumberyard. They
dashed into Mr. Bobbsey's office.

He and Sam Johnson were talking in low
tones. Both men had worried expressions. Nan
noticed this in spite of her excitement. But she
had no chance to ask if anything was wrong, for
Freddie cried out:

"Daddy, may we have the boat to go to Horseshoe Island tomorrow? The treasure's there—"

"Nan found the map in an old Spanish hat!"
Flossie said almost at the same time, and Bert
produced the chart.

As the children unfolded their story Mr.
Bobbsey and Sam's worried looks changed to
ones of astonishment.

"And we're going to wear pirate suits," Flossie
concluded. "Even Nan and I."

"The Lakeport buccaneers," Mr. Bobbsey
chuckled, then added, "I'll have the launch

ready for your island trip. I guess I can spare Sam to be pilot. Also, for such a special occasion, Jimmy, tomorrow will be a paid holiday for you."

The boy's face shone with delight, and Nan said, "Dad, you're a peach."

Flossie looked at Sam. "You'll have to be a dress-up pirate, too." She giggled.

Sam grinned widely. "I 'magine Dinah can fix me up somethin' to wear."

It was decided that the group would set out the next morning at eight-thirty. Then Jimmy went off with Sam to begin his afternoon's work in the yard. Nan, Flossie, and Bert hurried home to figure out the directions for locating the treasure on Horseshoe Island.

But Freddie lingered in his father's office. The little boy had not forgotten the model of the ancient Spanish ship in the Dodges' apartment. How he would love to have one like it! Maybe he could try to make a little ship of his own.

"Daddy," said Freddie. "I—I want to build something. It's a secret. Are there some small pieces of wood around that I could use?"

Mr. Bobbsey looked up from a sheaf of papers on his desk. He had been going through them slowly and frowning. But now he gave his son a smile. "I believe Mike can help you find some for your project," he said.

"Thanks, Daddy." Freddie hastened out into

the mill yard. As always, he was fascinated by the sounds and sights of the busy place.

Above him the tramways shook as the loaded carts rumbled along. The huge electric saws made a shrieking noise as they sliced through the wood. Freddie sniffed deeply of the pungent odor of sawdust and wood chips. Best of all he liked the shrill whistles of the boats when they pulled away from the dock with the lumber.

The little boy did not see Mike anywhere around. "He's probably inside the mill," Freddie thought. Impatient to start on his ship, he decided to look for the wood himself.

Freddie gazed at a high stack of loosely piled lumber near him. "There must be some small boards on top," he told himself. "I'll climb up and see."

He put the toe of his shoe on a projecting board and began to mount the pile. Up, up he went, and finally reached the top. But there were no boards small enough for his use up there. Disappointed, Freddie began to descend. This proved not so easy as going up had been.

All of a sudden the little boy felt the planks shift under his feet. The whole pile of lumber began to sway alarmingly.

Freddie fought down panic and gingerly stepped down to the next board. As he did, the huge stack of lumber collapsed, carrying Freddie with it!

CHAPTER VIII

A LUMBERYARD WIGWAM

BUMPITY-bump, Freddie was bounced from one board to another as the lumber pile clattered to the ground. Finally the little boy landed, sitting down hard.

"Oof!" gasped Freddie, the breath knocked out of him.

Otherwise he was unhurt. But he found himself inside a wigwam formed by some of the boards which had fallen in an upright position.

"How'll I ever get out?" Freddie asked himself worriedly. He dared not push against the planks, for fear they would topple over on him. There was no opening large enough for him to squeeze through.

"Mike! Mike!" he yelled as loudly as he could.

But the sound of his voice was drowned out by the mill-yard noises. Nevertheless, Freddie shouted until he was hoarse. No response came.

Although frightened, he determined to wait calmly until rescue arrived.

Freddie thought ruefully, "I should've asked Mike to find me the wood for my toy galleon."

As the minutes went by, and still no help came, Freddie worried anew. What if—what if nobody found him until tomorrow! Besides becoming very hungry, he might miss the pirate treasure hunt!

"I hope they don't go without me," the little boy thought. A big lump rose in his throat. He told himself sternly not to cry.

Instead, Freddie called again for help at the top of his lungs. "Mike—Sam—DADDY!"

But it was no use. Discouraged and tired, Freddie lay down as well as he could in his cramped quarters. Soon he fell fast asleep.

At the Bobbsey house, meanwhile, Flossie and the older twins were seated on the porch steps. Nan, in the middle, held the treasure map spread out on her lap.

Bert had a note pad and pencil. "Let's hope the code works for the directions," he said.

His sisters watched breathlessly as he copied the first row of numbers below the name Horseshoe Island: eight, seven, twenty-six, nine, seven. Bert quickly counted backward from Z to find the matching letters, and wrote them out.

"It spells 'Start'!" Flossie cried. "Let's do the next row, quick!"

With growing excitement the three carefully decoded the many rows of numbers on the map. It took some time but finally Bert copied the last word of the message.

"Boy!" he exclaimed. "These are nifty directions!"

At that moment the twins saw Charlie Mason coming down the street. Flossie stood up and called, "Charlie, hurry up! Jimmy's treasure is on Horseshoe Island, and we're going there tomorrow."

"Flossie, *shh!*" Nan warned suddenly. She had spotted Danny Rugg riding his bicycle in the street a few feet behind Charlie.

"Oh!" Flossie clapped her hand over her mouth.

Nan and Bert groaned. It was evident the bully had heard Flossie's words. A smug look came over his face and he rode off swiftly in the opposite direction.

"I'm awful sorry," Flossie said contritely to her brother and sister.

"Don't worry, honey," Nan reassured her, and Bert added, "We have the directions. Danny can't do much without them."

By now Charlie had joined the Bobbseys, and they told him of the day's events and the planned trip to Horseshoe Island.

"Can you be at Dad's dock by eight-thirty tomorrow?" Bert asked him.

"You bet I can!" Charlie said eagerly. "I have an old costume I'll put on." He grinned. "It's not exactly a pirate outfit, though."

Flossie went inside to telephone Johnnie Wilson and let him know about the trip. The little boy excitedly promised to meet them at the appointed time. He said he did not have a pirate costume either, but would wear something "special." Then he asked to speak to Freddie.

"Freddie isn't home," Flossie told him. "He's at the lumberyard."

After she hung up the phone, Flossie wondered what her twin could be working on.

"I guess it must be real 'portant," she decided, "he's been gone so long."

Rejoining the others, she found Bert reading aloud the treasure directions he had written out.

"Start at big rock southwest of island." Bert interrupted himself and pointed to a large circle on the map. "That must be the one," he said, and continued reading.

"Go into woods. Walk northeast fifty yards. Turn left at tall pine. Follow narrow trail west to patch of scrub oak. Over hill at right, walk west to third large rock. Turn left to cove. Turn left again. Walk along shore. Indian-head rock. Treasure six feet behind under large twisted tree."

"Oh, I can hardly wait until tomorrow!" Nan exclaimed, her brown eyes aglow.

Jubilantly the twins and Charlie studied the map and directions again. It was decided that their expedition should be kept as secret as possible.

"In case somebody's snooping around here," Bert said, "we'd better not put on our costumes until we get to the lumberyard." Everyone guessed that he meant Danny Rugg as one of the "snoopers."

"Good idea," agreed Charlie. "Say, have you seen that scar-faced man around?"

"Not since we chased him," Nan replied.

"I hope he's gone away," Flossie said vehemently, "and won't try to spy on Jimmy or us any more."

When Mrs. Bobbsey arrived home a short while later, the children showed her the results of their work on the map. "Why, how marvelous!" she praised them.

Dinah came outside just then. Hearing of the exciting plans, she chuckled. "I reckon even you pirates could eat some peanut cookies."

"You bet!"

She hustled inside and came back with a plate of freshly baked ones. As Flossie munched hers, she asked Dinah, "What kind of costume will you fix up for Sam?"

The cook's eyes twinkled merrily. "You'll see tomorrow," was all she would say.

Mrs. Bobbsey looked at her watch. "It's time

to start supper," she said. "Dad will be home shortly. Freddie must be waiting to come with him."

After Charlie left, the girls began to set the table. Bert was just about to take Snap for a walk when the telephone rang. He answered it.

"Hi, Dad!" said Bert. A moment later he gasped. "Freddie missing? But isn't he still at the yard? Oh. . . . Okay, we'll be right there."

Bert hung up and dashed into the kitchen. His mother asked quickly, "What's the matter?"

"Dad says they can't find Freddie anywhere at the yard. He was supposed to look for Mike to help him get some boards, but Mike hasn't seen him all afternoon. Nobody else has, either."

For a moment the family and Dinah could only stare at one another, shocked. Flossie's lower lip began to quiver. Was her twin lost—or hurt somewhere?

"Nan," Mrs. Bobbsey said, "before we leave, call up Johnnie and Freddie's other friends. Ask if they've seen him recently."

Nan rushed to do this, but returned to report that Freddie had not stopped at any of their homes.

"I didn't think so," said Mrs. Bobbsey, trying to be calm. "Freddie never leaves the yard without telling your father."

"Let's hurry and search with Daddy," Flossie urged tearfully.

The children and their mother climbed into the station wagon. Bert took Snap along. "We'll put him on the trail, too." Dinah said she would call the lumberyard office in case there was any news by phone.

In the meantime, Freddie Bobbsey was just waking up. He had slept so soundly that for a moment he thought he was home in bed. But the next second the little boy sat up and saw the wooden planks which held him prisoner.

"Why doesn't somebody find me?" Freddie

wondered with a sinking heart. He had no idea
how many hours had gone by. He became aware
then that the lumberyard noises had ceased. It
must be after closing time, he thought. And it
was dusky inside his plank wigwam. Was it sun-
set or midnight?

"Anyway, I'm awful hungry," he told himself
miserably. Another idea struck him. Perhaps
searchers had called for him while he was asleep,
and he had not heard them!

"Maybe Daddy and the others are still
around," Freddie murmured hopefully.

The little boy took a deep breath. He was
about to yell with all his might, when suddenly
he heard scratching and sniffing noises near his
lumber wigwam. Freddie felt a surge of joy. It
sounded like a dog! Snap, maybe!

If it were, then his family must be nearby!
Freddie again started to call out. At the same
moment, he heard the sound of footsteps. Then a
man's voice muttered crossly:

"Rags! Get out of there! We have no time for
games!"

Freddie's heart skipped a beat. "It's the scar-
faced man!" he thought.

CHAPTER IX

TREASURE HUNT COSTUMES

FREDDIE held his breath and listened intently. He could hear Rags sniffing and scratching around the tent of lumber. The dog's master muttered something to the animal, but Freddie could not make out the words.

His heart was pounding furiously. What was Mr. Scarface doing at the lumberyard? If only, thought Freddie, he could warn his father! Or the watchman! But he dared not call out.

Finally, the little boy heard the strange man say, "Come on, Rags. We're scramming out of here. Next time we'll come back when it's real dark."

To Freddie's relief, there came the sound of receding footsteps. Then all was quiet. He decided to wait a few more minutes before shouting for help.

"I wonder," mused Freddie worriedly, "what that man is after—and why he's coming back here when it's dark. Oh!" A sudden realization struck him. "That must mean it's still kind of daylight."

His legs and arms were cramped from sitting still for such a long time. He shifted around to a different position. At the same moment Freddie caught sight of something white sticking under one of the boards.

Curious, Freddie gently pulled the white object all the way out. It proved to be a bulky envelope which was torn open. Inside was a document of several pages. Freddie could not see it well enough to read the printing, but he could make out his father's name on the top page.

"This is funny," Freddie said to himself, puzzled.

He tucked the papers back into the envelope. Suddenly Freddie spotted another paper wedged under the same board. He pulled it out and looked closely at the single piece of paper. In spite of the dimness, he could see several curving lines sketched on it.

"Why!" he exclaimed aloud. "This looks sort of like Jimmy's treasure chart. Only it's smaller and it isn't on stiff paper."

The little boy studied the sheet again. Next to the curving lines were symbols similar to the ones he had seen on Jimmy's map. Several numbers were printed in the right-hand corner.

"But there are more numbers on Jimmy's

chart," Freddie observed to himself. "Maybe this map never got finished."

Again he pondered how the envelope and the sketch had become stuck beneath the board. "I'm sure they weren't here at first," Freddie thought.

Suddenly he remembered the scar-faced man. Could he have dropped the papers? But if so, how had he obtained the one bearing Mr. Bobbsey's name?

Freddie stuffed envelope and papers into his shirt and then shouted for help. Abruptly he stopped. The sound of running footsteps had come to his ears.

Freddie gulped. Was it Mr. Scarface? Then the little boy heard a dog barking. This time his heart gave a leap of joyful recognition.

"Snap!" Freddie cried. He put his face against a crack in the boards and called, "Snap! Snap! Here I am, boy!"

The barking grew louder and more frantic. The footsteps came nearer. "Freddie! Freddie!" It was Flossie's voice. "Where are you?"

Almost sobbing with relief, Freddie called out, "Under these boards."

Outside, Flossie exclaimed, "Oh, thank goodness we've found you!" Excitedly she summoned the other searchers.

Soon her parents, then Bert and Nan, followed by Jimmy Dodge, Sam, and Mike, the day watchman, raced up to the pile of fallen boards. Snap was running back and forth, wagging his tail furiously and sniffing.

Mrs. Bobbsey cried out, "Are you all right, Freddie?"

"Yes, Mother," came her son's reply. " 'Cept I'll sure be glad to get out of here."

In a matter of minutes the men and boys had carefully lifted the boards away from Freddie. The little boy rose stiffly to his feet and blinked his eyes. After an exchange of happy greetings and hugs all around, Freddie told the story of his mishap.

"You were very lucky to escape being hurt," his father remarked gravely.

"I'll say!" Mike declared, mopping his brow. "Next time you want to get any lumber around here, Freddie, be sure to look me up."

"I will," Freddie promised.

He learned that his family had searched practically every building and section of the lumberyard, including the docks.

"When we came to the lumber stacks," Bert said, "Snap picked up your trail."

"That's right," Flossie put in, patting the dog gratefully.

As the Bobbseys were leaving for home, Sam Johnson said he would stay awhile to finish up some chores.

"Don't forget the costume Dinah's fixing you

for the treasure hunt tomorrow," Nan reminded him.

Sam grinned. "I won't. Reckon it'll be some outfit!"

The Bobbseys and their friends climbed into the station wagon, and soon they were home again.

"Glory be!" cried Dinah, who had to hear the whole story of Freddie's adventure.

To celebrate the little boy's safe return, she made peach shortcake with whipped cream for dessert.

Freddie finished his second helping and grinned. "I guess I won't be hungry till tomorrow," he said, leaning back in his chair.

As he did he felt something crackle in his shirt front. Freddie gasped. The envelope and sketch! He had forgotten them in the excitement of being found. And he had forgotten something else, too. Quickly Freddie told of hearing Mr. Scarface and Rags while he was a prisoner beneath the boards.

"What!" Mr. Bobbsey exclaimed, and the others stared in astonishment.

"And," Freddie added, "I heard him say he's going to come back when it's dark."

All this time he had been pulling at the envelope and sketch to get them out. Now he succeeded and showed them to his father.

When Mr. Bobbsey saw the document, he exclaimed, "Why, this is a business contract that has been missing from my office. I have been looking all over for it."

"Is that why you seemed worried this afternoon?" Nan guessed.

Mr. Bobbsey nodded. "This contract is for a big job and means a lot to my business." He explained that he had left the envelope in his desk drawer the previous evening. "I'll keep it in the safe from now on, though."

The family went into the living room and continued to discuss the matter. With a worried look, Mrs. Bobbsey asked her husband, "Do you think that strange man took the contract?"

"It seems that way. If so, he must have been prowling around last night, and managed to sneak into my office." Mr. Bobbsey added that he would check with Alec, the night watchman at the yard. "I'll phone right now," he said, "and warn him to keep a sharp lookout tonight. And I'll call the police, too."

When Mr. Bobbsey came back, Nan said, "I guess Mr. Scarface thought something he wanted was in the envelope. When it turned out to be the contract, he came back after closing time and dropped it when his dog was acting up."

Mr. Bobbsey reported that Alec had not noticed or heard anything unusual at the lumberyard the night before.

"Mr. Scarface is a slick one," Bert remarked.

"I'm afraid he is," the twins' father agreed. "But the police are going to send out more patrol cars in an effort to spot the fellow."

"That's good," Flossie spoke up. "I hope they catch him and that mean old Rags, too."

Everyone felt puzzled about the sketch. They agreed with Freddie that because of the numbers and symbols it did resemble Jimmy Dodge's pirate chart.

"Maybe Mr. Scarface dropped it by mistake with Dad's contract," Bert ventured. He had been studying the piece of paper. "And, if this is a map," he said, "I wonder what the curving lines stand for."

The twins and their parents had to admit that they were stumped for an answer.

"One more mystery to work on," Nan declared.

Presently the children went to bed, but arose early, eager to start out on the treasure-hunting expedition.

"Did you finish Sam's costume?" Flossie asked Dinah after breakfast.

"I sure did," the cook replied with a broad smile. "Sam took it with him when he drove your daddy to the lumberyard."

The twins promised Dinah that they would take snapshots of the searching party in costume. Bert got his camera, then the twins went off in the station wagon with their mother.

When they arrived at Jimmy's house, the boy and his grandmother were waiting outside. Mrs. Dodge explained that she would keep Laddie with her that day.

"I think you'll have too full a boat for such a lively puppy," she said.

"Grandma's right," Jimmy agreed, then held up two large paper parcels. "These are the out-fits," he said with a grin and climbed into the back beside Bert.

"Wonderful!" Nan exclaimed. All the Bobb-seys thanked Mrs. Dodge for her work on the costumes.

"Oh, it was fun," she replied.

"We'll bring you back some pictures of us pi-rates," Flossie told her.

As they started away, the children and Mrs. Bobbsey waved good-by to Mrs. Dodge.

A little after eight-thirty, a colorfully attired group began assembling at the lumberyard dock. Mr. Bobbsey, who had come down to see the treasure seekers off, winked at his wife.

"I've never seen such an unusual crew, Mary," he said.

Mrs. Bobbsey laughed. "It's great."

Flossie and Freddie were wearing red- and green-striped shirts, purple breeches, and red bandannas on their curly hair.

Bert and Nan were dressed in white shirts and loose-fitting blue trousers with tight cuffs. Each had on a red neck scarf and black cocked hat. All the twins wore their own rain boots.

"Oh, look at Jimmy!" cried Flossie. "He's a real pirate chief!"

The twins applauded as their friend joined them. Jimmy wore black breeches, a short, red sleeveless velvet coat, black shirt, and wide-topped boots. On his head was the plumed Spanish prince's hat in which his map had been found.

"Avast, me hearties," he cried, making his voice as deep as he could. "Make ready to sail the seven seas and search for buried pieces of eight!"

Flossie giggled. "You really sound like a pirate chief."

"Let's call him Captain Jim," Freddie proposed.

Charlie Mason appeared next. He wore an old-time sailor suit, and a black patch over one eye.

"Boy!" he said. "Those get-ups you all have on are terrific."

Jimmy grinned. "That eye-patch makes you look fierce as a pirate."

Sam Johnson was the center of attention when he walked up to the dock. He had on bright yellow cotton trousers, cut off raggedly below the knees. A red shirt and head cloth with large gold hoops on his ears completed his outfit.

"You're a bee-*yoo*-ti-ful pirate," Flossie declared.

"Dinah sure got me up fancy!" Sam chuckled.

Everyone laughed, and Bert quickly took a picture of Sam. Then Mr. Bobbsey snapped several of the children.

Suddenly Nan gasped, "Oh, goodness! Here comes a monkey!"

CHAPTER X

HORSESHOE ISLAND

"A MONKEY?" everyone repeated and looked in the direction where Nan was staring.

Approaching the group on the dock was a small, brown, monkey-like creature with a long tail!

"My *stars!*" Sam Johnson burst out unbelievingly. "Where—"

The next moment he broke off and joined the others in uproarious laughter. The "monkey" was Johnnie Wilson! The little boy removed a mask and came up, grinning.

"Johnnie," gasped Flossie when she could stop laughing, "how can you be a monkey on a pirate trip?"

Johnnie was not discouraged. "Oh, monkeys live on pirates' islands, don't they, Jimmy?"

"I'm sure they do," Captain Jim replied with a chuckle.

"A monkey might be a lucky mascot to have

along," Mr. Bobbsey added, smiling, as he took a picture of the entire group.

Just then Mike Donovan came down to report that there had been no sign of any intruder during the night.

"Alec told me everything was quiet," the day watchman added. "But we'll keep our eyes open for anybody sneakin' around here."

The Bobbseys then quickly explained to Jimmy about Mr. Scarface's having been at the yard the previous afternoon.

"And we think he dropped the pirate map Freddie found," Flossie said.

"Maybe," Bert put in, "it isn't a pirate map. But it has some numbers and symbols like yours, Jimmy."

Jimmy was puzzled. "That's funny," he remarked. "I'd like to see it when we get back."

Mike then wished the children luck and went off.

"Let's go!" Bert urged, and everyone walked onto the dock, where the lumberyard motor launch, the *Tall Timber,* was waiting. Sam, carrying two cardboard boxes, stepped in first.

"This is a neat boat," said Jimmy admiringly as he clambered aboard.

"And big, too," Charlie added. "There's plenty of room for all eight of us."

Sam took the wheel, and the twins and their friends seated themselves in the back behind the

little cabin. Mr. Bobbsey then handed down
shovels and spades for the children to use on
Horseshoe Island. Bert and Jimmy cast off the
lines, and the *Tall Timber* pulled away from
the dock. Her passengers waved to Mr. and Mrs.
Bobbsey, who called out:

"Happy treasure hunting to Captain Jim's
expedition!"

The children were in high spirits as the launch
picked up speed and headed onto Lake Metoka.
A fresh breeze whipped up little waves, which
glittered in the bright morning sunshine.

Flossie curiously eyed the two boxes which
Sam had set down on the deck near him. "Sam,"

she called above the noise of the motor, "what's inside the boxes?"

The pilot turned his head slightly and gave a mysterious grin. "Oh, you all'll find out in a few hours."

"Can't you give us a little hint?" Freddie begged.

"Well, I'll tell you this much," Sam replied. "Those boxes have somethin' inside that Dinah thought a body might want after hard huntin' for treasure."

"I know!" Johnnie piped up. "Food!"

"You guessed it," Sam admitted.

"Three cheers for Dinah!" Bert said. "We sure *will* be hungry for some lunch."

"An island pirate picnic, goody!" Flossie exclaimed.

Presently Bert, Jimmy, and Charlie went up to Sam at the wheel.

"I think we start turning north toward Belleville now," Bert said.

"Right," Charlie agreed. "Seems to me Horseshoe Island is near the middle of the lake."

Sam swung the launch northward, then offered the wheel to Jimmy. "Straight ahead, Cap'n," said the kindly man.

Jimmy was delighted. Eagerly he gripped the wheel and kept the *Tall Timber* on a steady course. After a while Bert and Charlie took turns as pilots.

"Let's go over the directions again," Bert suggested when the three boys sat down once more.

"Okay." Jimmy pulled the paper from his shirt pocket. He unfolded the sheet and held it up.

Suddenly a strong puff of wind almost blew Jimmy's plumed hat off. He grabbed it, but at the same moment the paper slipped from his hand.

"Oh!" he gasped.

The paper fluttered over the children's heads for a moment, then sailed toward the water. Quick as a wink Johnnie hopped onto the seat, reached out, and grasped it just in time.

"Great catch!" Bert praised the little boy.

"I'll say," Charlie echoed.

"You really are our monkey mascot," Jimmy added. "We'd have had to decipher the code over again without these directions."

"Let's go inside the cabin out of the wind," Nan suggested.

The children went into the enclosed section. They sat down on the benches which ran along the sides.

"I'm glad," said Freddie, peering at the directions, "that it says where to start looking for the treasure."

"Yes," agreed Flossie, "it will be easy to find the big rock."

"Unless," Jimmy said, "it's not there now."

Flossie spoke up, looking up and down the beach. There was no one in sight.

"Well, we can get more searching done if there aren't any people around," said Charlie.

In another minute Jimmy brought the *Tall Timber* alongside the rickety pier. The launch was quickly tied to one of the few remaining posts, close to shore.

Sam and the older boys leaped across the small stretch of water onto the beach. They pulled the boat near enough so that the others could hop out easily.

Nan held the measuring tape in readiness. Jimmy had the compass and directions.

The twins' hearts beat faster. Would they find Jimmy's hidden box of treasure?

CHAPTER XI

THE BURIED CHEST

"OOH!" Flossie spoke in an awed voice. "How still it is!"

"Yes," Nan agreed. "This island certainly seems deserted."

"Look how tall those trees are way back there!" said Bert. "It's a regular forest!"

Sam had decided he would stay near the launch for a while. "I'll try some fishing for our dinner," he said. "Brought my hand line along. But don't go into the woods without me."

"Okay," Bert promised.

"First," said Jimmy, "we look for the big rock." The boys picked up their shovels, and all the children set out along the shore to the southwest.

As they passed a grassy knoll at the edge of the woods, Nan remarked, "That would be a good place to eat our lunch."

"Right," said Charlie. "If we find the treasure we can come back here and celebrate."

The "pirate" expedition trooped on across the sand. They came finally to the inlet and walked around it.

"Whew!" Charlie exclaimed. "Some hike!"

"We're at the southwest part of the shore now," said Jimmy.

The children's eyes scanned the beach from left to right as they continued. After a while Johnnie said, "We haven't come to any big rocks."

The searchers paused to catch their breath.

"Of course, the directions don't say the rock is actually on the *beach*," Bert remarked.

Jimmy nodded. "And I can't tell from the circle on the map, either."

He suggested they divide forces for their hunt. He, Charlie, and Johnnie would keep looking along the beach. The twins would search farther inland among the undergrowth bordering the sand.

"We'll shout if we see the rock," said Charlie.

"And I'll blow my whistle three times if we do," Freddie added.

Presently the Bobbseys were pushing their way through a tangle of milkweed and scrubby bushes.

"Ow!" Flossie cried out as she pulled off a

burr which had caught on her breeches. "It feels like a million needles."

The twins plodded on determinedly. Nan sighed. "Maybe Jimmy was right about the rock not being here any more," she said.

"Oh dear," Flossie wailed, "then we won't know where to begin."

Suddenly Bert spotted a rounded, moss-covered hillock about ten yards ahead. "I'll climb up there and have a look," he said, and ran toward the hillock.

He started upward. To Bert's surprise, the surface was hard and slippery and he could not gain a foothold.

"Hey," Bert called to the others, "this feels like rock underneath."

Nan, Flossie, and Freddie hurried to his side. "Do you think—" Nan began, her eyes widening.

Bert picked up a stick and scraped away some of the moss. Gray-white stone was revealed.

"The big rock!" Freddie cried out.

"Sure. This moss has grown over it since Jimmy and Captain Dodge came here," Bert reasoned. "No wonder we had trouble spotting it."

The twins ran their hands over the surface of the "hill" and made certain it was entirely of stone.

"Let's signal the others," Freddie urged.

Jubilantly he blew his fireman's whistle—once, twice, three times. In a short while the Bobbseys heard running footsteps. Jimmy, Charlie, and Johnnie came into view, racing as fast as they could through the underbrush.

"You—you've found the big rock?" Jimmy burst out breathlessly.

The twins pointed to the hill-like formation, and Flossie said, "Bert found it when he tried to climb up."

The three boys were amazed. They felt positive this was the starting point indicated on Jimmy's map.

"Which way now, Captain Jim?" Bert asked eagerly.

Jimmy glanced at the instructions. "Northeast into woods for fifty yards," he replied, "to the tall pine. Then we turn left."

He consulted the compass and pointed out the direction.

"I'll get Sam," Bert said. "We'll meet you at the woods." He dashed off.

Soon he and Sam reached the others, who stood waiting at the edge of the wooded area. Flossie peered among the trees.

"It's sort of dark," she said nervously.

The foliage was so dense that very little sunshine filtered through the leaves. This made the woods look rather gloomy.

Jimmy had pushed in. "I see a little path

over there," he pointed out. "And it leads to the northeast."

"Good. Let's mark off the fifty yards," Bert said. "Fifty feet three times should bring us to the tall pine."

Nan offered to hold the tape spool while the older boys measured. "When fifty feet runs out," she said, "Freddie can blow his whistle."

"Okay," Jimmy agreed. "Then we'll wait till you catch up."

He pulled out the tape and began unreeling it. Bert and Charlie, carrying some of the shovels, followed him along the path into the woods. The three were soon out of sight among the trees. Sam remained with Nan and the younger children.

They watched closely as the tape steadily unwound. Freddie had his whistle ready and counted aloud:

"Thirty feet . . . thirty-five . . . forty . . . forty-five . . ."

"Fifty!" Flossie sang out and Freddie blew loudly on his whistle.

"Here we go!" Sam said.

He and the four children picked up the remaining spades and hurried into the woods.

Another measurement was made, then another. At the end of the third the group came to the end of the path. They found themselves in a small clearing, and gazed about, perplexed.

Before them stood several tall pines in a row.

"How do we know which tree is the right one?" Freddie voiced the question in everyone's mind.

Jimmy got out the directions and his chart. "Well," he said after a moment, "there's only one big X on the map. So Dad must have meant just one pine tree." Then he glanced at the next direction and read, "Follow narrow trail west to patch of scrub oak."

Immediately the treasure hunters explored the area near the pines. But there was no sign of a narrow trail. Sam paused and pushed back his headcloth.

"Looks like that old trail's been swallowed up," he declared.

"I'm afraid so," Nan spoke up. "It's probably overgrown by now."

Freddie and Johnnie had a plan. They would climb two maple trees standing near the pines. "Maybe we can tell if there's any trail to the left," Freddie said.

"All right. But don't go too high," Nan cautioned.

Sam boosted Freddie to the lowest limb of one maple, and Bert helped Johnnie up. The little boys pulled themselves to the next branch.

Impulsively Freddie called to his friend, "I'll bet I can climb faster than you even if you are a monkey!"

"A pirate can't climb fast," Johnnie scoffed.

"We'll see!" Freddie scrambled to the branch above him. Johnnie did the same.

In their race, the "pirate" and the "monkey" forgot Nan's warning. Higher and faster they clambered upward.

"Hey!" Sam shouted to them. "That's far enough."

Just then there was a sharp *crack* from Johnnie's tree. Those standing below gasped. The little boy stood halfway out on a rotted limb. It was slowly splintering beneath his feet!

"Johnnie!" Bert cried. "Get back near the tree trunk quick!"

Johnnie clung to the branch above and lifted his feet. Hand over hand, he swung himself back to the trunk of the maple. He managed to step onto another limb just as the rotted one broke off and crashed to the ground.

"Oh, thank goodness!" Nan and the others gave sighs of relief.

"You two had better climb down," Jimmy called. "We'll figure out some other way."

Meekly the tree climbers descended. When they were safely on the ground, Freddie said:

"I'm sorry, Johnnie. I won't race you up trees any more."

Johnnie grinned. "If I was a real monkey, I would've won," he retorted.

After a short conference on their next move, the group came to a decision. Jimmy had pointed out that the pine tree in the middle looked a bit taller than the others.

"Let's try it," Bert said.

The searchers turned to the left of the center pine. Soon they were tramping through thick underbrush to the west. For a while the little procession continued in silence. Suddenly Jimmy, who was in the lead, gave a shout.

"I think I've found the trail—or what used to be one."

The others quickly caught up to him. Jimmy pointed straight ahead. Definitely a narrow line of underbrush was much shorter than that on either side. With renewed hope the children and Sam pressed on. Presently they observed that the trees were diminishing in height.

In another minute the group came out into the bright sunshine. Directly in front of them was a patch of stunted trees.

"The scrub oaks!" Bert exclaimed.

"What's next, Captain Jim?" asked Freddie eagerly.

"Over that hill to the right," Jimmy replied, "and west to the third large rock."

He led the others up a hilly section. As they came down the other side, Flossie spied a big jagged stone jutting out of the ground. "There's one rock!"

About ten yards farther on Bert saw the second rock, partially hidden by tall grass. Nan detected the third one through a clump of wild blackberry bushes.

"Now," Jimmy directed, "we turn left and look for a cove."

Although there was no path now, the group found the going much easier. There was little underbrush and trees grew far apart. Gradually the land sloped upward.

Reaching the top, the Bobbseys and their friends gazed down. Below them lay a small cove, blue and shining.

Excitedly Sam and the children descended the sandy slope toward it.

Reaching the cove, Jimmy looked at his compass. "We're on the north shore of Horseshoe Island," he told the others.

"Boy, we've walked the whole way across," Charlie remarked.

Bert looked at the directions over Jimmy's shoulder. "Another left turn here," he said. "Then we follow the shore till we come to an Indian-head rock."

"And the treasure's six feet behind it under a large twisted tree," Jimmy finished.

Off marched the treasure hunters along the white sand. They walked for a quarter of a mile, then came to an abrupt halt. A huge mass of boulders blocked their path.

"We'll have to wade around it," said Bert, and the searchers splashed through the shallow water.

"Good thing we all wore boots," Sam remarked. He and the children skirted the rocky

pile and stepped back onto shore. Suddenly they
stopped.

"The Indian-head!" Flossie shrieked, pointing.

On the sand about fifteen yards ahead of them

lay a tremendous rock. Its outline formed the rugged profile of an Indian, even to his feathered headdress!

Freddie gave a whoop of joy. "And there's the twisted tree."

A gnarled, wind-swept pine stood behind the rock at the edge of an evergreen grove. With excited cries the children trooped over to the pine. Bert and Jimmy quickly measured the distance from tree to rock.

"Six feet," Jimmy announced triumphantly. "Let's dig!"

Sam and the children each chose a spot near the tree. For several minutes there was only the sound of shovels and spades crunching into sandy soil.

Suddenly a loud metallic *clank* was heard. "I've hit something," Jimmy cried out.

The others ran to his side and peered into the hole he had dug. Plainly visible was an iron lid. Sam, Bert, and Charlie helped dig away the surrounding soil. Everyone gasped as a large iron chest came into view.

"Oh, Jimmy!" Nan exclaimed. "Your treasure!"

The boys bent to lift out the chest.

"Leave that alone!" thundered a voice behind them.

CHAPTER XII

LITTLE ACTORS

THE TWINS and their friends jumped up, startled. Again the strange voice came:

"Leave that chest alone!"

A man emerged from the evergreen grove and strode toward the group. He wore a green beret and carried a megaphone.

"What do you think you're doing?" he demanded. "Don't you—"

He stopped speaking abruptly as he reached the children. His angry expression changed to one of amazement.

At the same time Flossie cried out, "You're Mr. Roland, the movie man."

"Indeed I am," he replied, smiling now. "I'm here to shoot some scenes for my latest movie. You little pirates are the Bobbsey twins and Jimmy Dodge. I never forget a name." He winked at Freddie. "Tried out for any more train robbery films lately?"

"No, Mr. Roland," the little boy giggled.

Bert spoke up. "We've been hunting for Jimmy's buried treasure, and we just found it." He introduced Charlie, Johnnie, and Sam.

Mr. Roland glanced from the iron chest to the children. "This is an amazing coincidence. I'm sorry to spoil your game," he said, "but this particular chest belongs to our movie company."

"Oh!" Jimmy burst out in dismay. "You see, Mr. Roland, we're not just playing a game. My father, a sea captain who's been missing since his ship was wrecked, hid this box many years ago on my birthday for me to try to find later."

"How very interesting!" the director said. "Unusual, too." After hearing the full story and being shown the treasure chart, Mr. Roland expressed his sympathy about Captain Dodge. "I hope you'll receive good news of your father."

The director then gave a sigh. "I hate to see you disappointed in your search, but this iron chest is one of our props for a scene in our film."

Mr. Roland stooped down and flung back the lid of the chest. The iron box was empty! The twins' hearts sank, and Sam shook his head sympathetically.

But Jimmy was not ready to give up. "My treasure might still be buried in this spot, only deeper."

"That's the spirit." Mr. Roland put a hand on Jimmy's shoulder. "Why not try digging again?"

"Oh, may we?" Nan asked, cheering up.

"Sure," said the director. "We won't be ready to shoot our treasure sequence until tomorrow. My crew are setting up other props. We brought the stuff over by launch this morning."

"Why did you decide on Horseshoe Island for your movie scene?" Bert asked.

The director explained that he had heard of the unusual Indian-head rock, and thought it would be an effective background. "And of course," he added, "this twisted pine is an ideal treasure spot in our picture. Jimmy's dad must have thought so, too."

"Is your picture going to be about pirates?" Charlie guessed.

"That's right," said Mr. Roland. "It's called *The Vanishing Buccaneer*. It's the story of pirates who used to range the Virginia coast."

The director paused and looked at the children with twinkling eyes. "Say," he exclaimed, "I have an idea. I'd like to shoot a test scene. Would you help me by being in it and dig for Jimmy's treasure at the same time?"

"Oh boy!" Freddie exclaimed. "That's neat!"

Mr. Roland said this would give him a chance to figure out the best camera angles to use for *The Vanishing Buccaneer* scenes.

"But how will we act?" Flossie wanted to know.

"Don't worry about that." Mr. Roland smiled.

"Just talk and do what you've been doing."

"It sounds like fun," Jimmy spoke up.

Mr. Roland put his megaphone to his lips and summoned his crew. Soon six men came out of the grove, where certain equipment was being set up.

"Yes, boss. What—" one of the men started to ask. When he saw the costumed group, his jaw dropped, and the other men stared.

Mr. Roland grinned. "It's okay, boys," he said. "This little expedition is going to do a test scene for us by digging for a *real* buried treasure. Tell John to bring a camera."

He introduced the twins and their friends to his assistants and explained why they had come to Horseshoe Island.

"Say, that's a terrific story," commented one of the men.

The man called John arrived with a camera and set it up at one side of the twisted pine. Then the large iron chest was removed.

"Now," Mr. Roland said briskly, "everybody set? Sam and you boys, have your shovels ready. Nan and Flossie, begin walking around. After a little while, Bert and Freddie, give your sisters a turn digging."

Excitedly the children took their places. Jimmy stood with his shovel poised at the spot where he had dug before. Mr. Roland held up his hand.

"Wait!" he said. "I think a good opening shot would be Jimmy studying his father's chart before the digging starts."

Jimmy pulled out the map and scanned it.

"Fine, fine." Mr. Roland signaled the cameraman. "Here we go. *Action!*"

The camera whirred. Jimmy continued looking at the chart for half a minute. Then he put it away and said clearly:

"According to Dad's map, the treasure *must* be here."

"We'll dig some more," Freddie spoke up loudly. He enjoyed making a movie scene even though it was only a test.

The shovels flew as Sam and the boys dug furiously. Nan and Flossie were not pretending when they looked on with keen interest. The girls walked about, pausing to watch each digger.

"We just *have* to find the chest Captain Dodge buried!" Flossie declared dramatically.

"Yes, and soon," Nan replied.

They approached Bert and Freddie, who handed them the shovels.

"Dig away, pirate Nan and pirate Flossie," Bert encouraged.

The girls determinedly dug as deep as they could. At this moment a resounding noise of metal striking metal came to everyone's ears.

"I—I've struck something!" Jimmy called out excitedly.

His companions rushed over. Jimmy was scraping away the soil from a rectangular-shaped piece of iron.

"It looks like a lid," Freddie cried, dancing about.

Sam and the other boys joined Jimmy in uncovering the metal object. Soon a chest, much smaller than the first one they had found, was revealed.

"I—I'll try my key," Jimmy said tensely, as he and Bert lifted the chest onto level ground.

Jimmy bent down and fitted a small wrought-iron key into the lock. He turned it carefully, then tugged at the lid of the box.

"It's opening!" Flossie squealed.

The onlookers, in a semicircle behind Jimmy, held their breath. The boy reached into the chest and drew out an envelope.

"It's addressed to me," Jimmy murmured, "in Dad's handwriting!"

"See what's inside," Freddie urged.

Carefully Jimmy slit the envelope with his finger. He removed the contents—a twenty-dollar bill, four one-dollar bills, and a folded piece of paper. Jimmy straightened out the white sheet.

"A note from Dad," he told the others.

"May we hear what it says?" Nan asked softly.

Jimmy nodded. Clearing his throat, he read:

"This treasure box is buried on my son's

seventh birthday. It is to be discovered and opened by him on his thirteenth birthday. The twenty dollars is to be deposited in the Belleville bank and the four dollars he may spend as he wishes. He has all my love. Signed, *Henry A. Dodge.*"

Everyone, deeply touched, was silent for a long moment. Jimmy was trying hard to hide his feelings. Finally he looked up at the others.

"Thank you all for helping me find my treasure," he said simply, then smiled at the twins. "And I'll never forget all you Bobbseys have done for me."

"Oh, it's been a wonderful treasure hunt," Nan cried out happily.

"It sure has been," Sam added.

Suddenly Mr. Roland said, "Cut!"

"Oh!" gasped Flossie. "I forgot we were in a movie."

Mr. Roland and his crew came forward and heartily congratulated Jimmy on his discovery. Then the director said, "This sequence is much too good to be only a test. In fact, it has given me an idea."

He excused himself and consulted with the cameraman and other technicians in a low tone. Meanwhile Jimmy put his father's note and the money into the metal chest and locked it.

Then Mr. Roland came back. "With your permission, Captain Jimmy and crew, I'd like to put your whole treasure search on film. Would you mind retracing your trip across Horseshoe Island?"

The director added that he thought the children's "pirate" hunt would be an appealing special feature. "I'm sure," he said, "that people in Lakeport and other towns around here would enjoy seeing it on their local screens."

For a moment the children were too overwhelmed to speak. Then Nan exclaimed, "How thrilling to be in a movie, and a true one, too!"

"Of course," Mr. Roland said, "you'll each receive payment for taking part. I'll mail a check and a letter to your families, which they can sign permitting me to release the picture."

"Will we go back and start over again on the south shore?" Charlie wanted to know.

Mr. Roland smiled. "Oh no. We'll shoot each step of your trip in reverse. We already have the last scene of Jimmy finding the chest. When the final picture is made, we'll put the scenes in the correct order."

Instructions were given to the cameramen and treasure hunters. One of the crew carried the treasure chest out of the camera's range. With Jimmy referring to his map, the group made their way back little by little to their starting point. Being more familiar with the route, they made much quicker progress.

Finally, what would be the first scene in the picture was shot. The group acted out the landing on Horseshoe Island in the *Tall Timber*.

"A really excellent performance." Mr. Roland praised the Bobbseys and their friends. "I'm going to rush your little movie through for showing. Look for it soon."

"What will it be called?" Flossie asked.

"Suppose you decide," Mr. Roland suggested.

"Let's call it 'Captain Jimmy's Island Treasure,'" Freddie replied promptly.

Everyone agreed this was a fine title. Mr. Roland and his crewmen then said they must get back to their other job. They shook hands. The children waved good-by until the men were lost to view.

"Everything's been so exciting," Nan declared. "I forgot all about lunch."

In a short while the group was seated on the grassy knoll, eating the delicious picnic food.

"Boy! Wait'll everybody at home hears Jimmy found his treasure," Bert said, "and that we're all going to be in a movie."

"Two big surprises," Flossie said happily.

Sam grinned. "Bet Dinah never thought she'd be seein' me in a *movin'* picture." Everyone laughed.

Suddenly Freddie cried, "I hear a boat motor."

They all listened. The sound grew louder, then a small launch appeared and headed toward the little pier. There was a man at the wheel, and a boy was perched in the prow.

"Oh dear!" exclaimed Nan. "It's Danny Rugg!"

CHAPTER XIII

A MYSTERY MAP

WHEN they recognized Danny Rugg in the oncoming motor boat, the Bobbseys decided to pay no attention to him and turned back to their picnic. But as soon as the boat was moored, Danny spotted the group on the knoll.

"Hey, you Bobbseys!" he cried, running up to them. "And I know you, Jimmy Dodge, and Charlie and Johnnie, even if you are all dressed up in those crazy outfits. You'd better get off my Uncle Bill's property. He's in the boat. I told him you'd be here digging up his land on a silly treasure hunt."

Bert sprang to his feet. "Your uncle owns Horseshoe Island?" he demanded in astonishment.

"Well, some of it, and he doesn't like trespassers," Danny said loudly. "You'd better leave before he throws you off."

The twins did not know whether to believe the bully or not.

"We certainly didn't know this was private property," Nan said. "If it is, we'll apologize to your uncle and leave."

Bert noticed that Danny's uncle had started along the shore in the opposite direction.

"Call him back," Bert urged. "I want to tell him we weren't doing any harm."

Danny hesitated, then said lamely, "He's too far away now. But you just better beat it," the bully blustered. "Uncle Bill's going to let a movie company use his property. They won't want you kids around here."

He dashed off after his uncle. The children and Sam laughed, and Charlie said with a chuckle, "Won't Danny be surprised when he learns the truth?"

"I don't believe his uncle owns any of this island," Johnnie spoke up.

"Let's forget Danny and start for home," Nan suggested.

Everyone helped clean up the picnic spot. Sam and the boys carried the shovels and spades and Jimmy's treasure chest onto the *Tall Timber*. The group had just gone aboard the launch when they saw Danny and his uncle returning along the shore.

"Now we'll see if Danny's threats come true," said Bert as the two approached.

Danny was scowling. To the twins' surprise he remained sullenly silent. But his uncle, a tall man with a twinkle in his blue eyes, greeted the group with a friendly smile.

"Well," he said, "I hear you buccaneers have had a successful search today."

"Oh, yes," Flossie replied.

Danny's uncle added, "I'll certainly come to see Mr. Roland's movie of your treasure expedition."

Jimmy now stepped forward. "I'm sorry if we were trespassing."

"Trespassing?" echoed the man with a puzzled look.

"Don't you own some land on this island?" Bert asked him.

"Why, no," Danny's uncle replied. "I help supervise this county property and give permission for its use in special projects."

"Like making movies?" Freddie inquired. "That's right."

The Bobbseys did not wish to tell tales on Danny, so they kept quiet about his boastful claim. But Bert asked the bully with a grin, "Coming to see Jimmy's picture?"

Danny did not reply and scowled more deeply than ever. Then his Uncle Bill said, "We must be off. Good-by."

With a wave he stepped into his launch. Danny followed quickly. The craft sped off.

"Wow!" Johnnie exclaimed. "Danny sure doesn't take after his uncle!"

Finally the *Tall Timber* and its passengers were headed toward Lakeport. Jimmy glanced back at Horseshoe Island, green and beautiful in the afternoon sunlight.

"This has been a swell day," he said, holding his treasure chest tightly. His companions all agreed that it had been wonderful indeed.

When the launch came in sight of the Lakeport wharf, Nan shaded her eyes. "There are Mother and Dad on the dock," she said. "Oh, and your grandmother is with them, Jimmy."

"And Laddie, too!" exclaimed Freddie.

The minute Sam had moored the launch, the children hopped off.

"We found it, Grandma!" Jimmy cried, running up to her with the chest in his hands. "Here's the treasure—a note from Dad with twenty dollars for the bank and four dollars for me to spend."

Mrs. Dodge put her arms about Jimmy's shoulders and smiled. "Oh, what a grand surprise!"

Laddie, as if sensing his young master's happiness, leaped up joyfully and licked Jimmy's hands. Then suddenly the boy looked worried. "Grandma, was there any trouble at the shop?"

Mr. Bobbsey answered, "We thought your grandmother should be here to welcome the expedition, Jimmy. She was able to get away from her work early. And now I'd like to extend my congratulations."

The boy's face shone. "Thank you, sir. But I couldn't have done it without such a terrific crew."

"You found the treasure yourself," Bert reminded his friend with a smile.

By that time Charlie and Johnnie's families had arrived to pick them up. After more excited congratulations, the twins and their friends hastened to change into regular clothes in rooms at the lumberyard. The pirate costumes were packed up once more.

Charlie and Johnnie then said good-by to the others. "See you in the movies!" they called to the twins from their cars.

"And you, too!" Bert called back with a grin.

The twins' parents and Mrs. Dodge looked

mystified. Nan's eyes sparkled, and she said, "Oh, we have so much to tell it's hard to know where to begin."

Mrs. Bobbsey smiled. She suggested that Mrs. Dodge and Jimmy join the family for supper. "Then we'll have a good chance to hear all about the Horseshoe Island adventurers."

Jimmy and his grandmother gladly accepted the invitation. Everyone piled into the station wagon, and Sam drove home.

Later at the dinner table, the grown-ups listened in amazement to the children's story. When Jimmy told of the dramatic moment when his spade hit the real treasure box, Dinah paused with a plate of muffins in her hand.

"I sure can't wait till I see that part in the movie," she declared. "And to think my Sam's in the picture!"

"He was good, too," Flossie piped up.

The twins then explained that Mr. Roland would send letters for their parents and Jimmy's grandmother to sign.

"So it will be all right to show the movie," Bert explained.

Flossie sighed. "The treasure hunt on Horseshoe Island was such fun," she said wistfully, "I wish we could find your other maps, Jimmy."

"We'll go on a detecting trip for them tomorrow," Bert announced.

"Let's," Nan and the small twins agreed.

"But where else would the maps be?" Jimmy mused. "We looked all through our trunks and boxes in the attic when we found my first map."

Bert said the twins would think very hard about this. "We'll try to figure out by morning what to do."

"I'm sure you'll think of something we haven't," Mrs. Dodge spoke up, smiling.

Jimmy announced that he would not accompany the twins on their sleuthing. He turned to Mr. Bobbsey.

"I had such a grand day off," Jimmy said, "I want to work full-time tomorrow to make up for it."

Mr. Bobbsey nodded and said he appreciated Jimmy's willingness. "I'll accept your offer," he added. "We do have plenty of work to be done at the yard."

After dessert everyone arose from the table. Bert asked his father if there had been any further signs of Mr. Scarface or his dog. Mr. Bobbsey shook his head. "And no word from the police on him, either."

"I'll show you that map Freddie found," Bert said to Jimmy.

The Bobbseys and their guests gathered in the living room. Bert handed Jimmy the mysterious sketch. The boy examined it closely, turning the paper in all directions.

Finally Jimmy looked up at the others, a

startled expression in his eyes. "I—I think this *is* part of a map," he said slowly. "And it's like the one Dad made for my Pacific island treasure!"

CHAPTER XIV

BICYCLE DETECTIVES

"OH, JIMMY!" Nan cried, as the Bobbseys and Mrs. Dodge stared at the sketch. "You mean someone may have copied the chart your dad made?"

"Or started to," Jimmy said. Excitedly he pointed to the curving lines on the paper. "I remember these stand for the Pacific coastline of South America. And this little dot to the left is an island."

"Probably the one your big treasure is on!" Bert guessed.

Jimmy nodded. "But of course I could tell for sure if I saw my own chart," he said. "There were lots more code numbers and symbols than these on it. So this one wouldn't do any good in finding the treasure."

"I wonder who wanted to copy my son's map?" Mrs. Dodge said.

Bert snapped his fingers. "I'm sure it was Mr. Scarface who dropped this paper."

"And," Nan broke in, "that would almost prove he's after Jimmy's South American treasure. You were right, Bert. He must have found out it's valuable!"

"And," Bert added, "what he's been looking for is the real chart so he can get the rest of the directions and try to decode them."

Mr. Bobbsey nodded. "Since Jimmy's working at the yard, the fellow probably thought the chart might be in my office. That's why he took the envelope from my desk on his first visit."

"Sure," Bert said, his mind racing. "If our hunch is right, it would explain why Mr. Scarface has been trailing Jimmy—and watching our house, too."

Flossie was thinking very hard. Now she said to Jimmy, "Do you suppose he stole the map from your daddy to copy and something happened so he couldn't finish and—"

The little girl stopped. Everyone was staring at her intently.

"What's the matter?" she asked.

"Flossie!" Bert exclaimed. "You've thought of the most important clue of all. Mr. Scarface must have known Captain Dodge if he took the map."

"Gracious!" Jimmy's grandmother looked startled. "In that case, this man somehow learned of my son's plan before the chart was mailed to Jimmy and before the shipwreck."

Jimmy spoke up eagerly. "Mr. Scarface may be a thief. But I'd like to ask him if he knows anything about Dad."

"I never thought I'd want to see that strange man again," Nan said. "But I guess he could answer a lot of questions."

"Sure," Bert said, then added, "He'll probably stay in hiding for a while if he thinks we've found his map and suspect him."

Mrs. Dodge shook her head in wonderment. "You twins are certainly good detectives to figure all this out."

Nan smiled. "We'll do our best to put more pieces of the puzzle together."

In a little while Jimmy and his grandmother rose to leave. Again they thanked the Bobbsey family for all they had done.

"Wasn't it a fine day?" Flossie spoke up. "I just loved the treasure hunt."

Mr. Bobbsey drove the Dodges and Laddie home. The twins went to bed immediately, their heads whirling with thoughts of their recent adventure.

When the children came downstairs next morning, they found their father reading a letter. He looked up at them and grinned.

"Three guesses who sent this?" he said teasingly.

"Mr. Roland!" chorused the twins.

"Right the first time." Mr. Bobbsey turned to

his wife. "Sounds fine to me, Mary. Shall we sign this release?"

Mrs. Bobbsey read it and smiled. Then she put her signature on it.

Flossie clapped her hands. "Goody! Then Mr. Roland can start our movie right away."

Mr. Bobbsey then showed the twins a check which had come with the letter. "This money is for all of you," he said.

The check was passed around. Freddie's eyes grew large when he saw it. "Boy!" he exclaimed. "That would make a lot of pennies for my bank."

"Yes," agreed Mrs. Bobbsey, and said she would put it in the twins' savings accounts.

At once Nan spoke up. "I'd like to give my share to Jimmy. He and his grandmother really need money."

"I'll give mine, too," said Bert. "After all, it really came to us because of Jimmy's treasure."

"Me, too," Freddie spoke up.

"And I want Jimmy to use mine," said Flossie.

Mr. and Mrs. Bobbsey looked at their children fondly. "I'm proud of you," the twins' father said, and their mother added, "I'm so glad you thought of it. Jimmy is a fine boy and deserves the reward."

She suggested that they drive Jimmy to the Belleville bank the next day. "He can open his own account and deposit the money along with the twenty dollars his father gave him."

"Neat," said Bert.

"I'll stop and tell him on my way to the office," Mr. Bobbsey offered. "But I guess your mother will have to make the trip. I'll be tied up."

Just as the family finished breakfast, Dinah and Sam came into the room. Pleased smiles covered their faces. "Got my movie check here," Sam announced, displaying an envelope.

"And," Dinah said, "Sam's decided to spend his in a special way."

Sam nodded. "I—I figure Jimmy Dodge ought to have this money. So will you please give it to him, Mr. Bobbsey?"

"Why, Sam, I'd be very glad to."

"Say," Bert spoke up, "tomorrow let's give all the checks to Jimmy as a big surprise. Dad, don't tell him today about the money."

This was agreed upon. Then Mr. Bobbsey and Sam left for the yard. The twins tidied their rooms. When they had finished, all four were eager to do some sleuthing in connection with the missing maps.

"Where'll we go first?" Flossie asked.

Bert proposed that they ride their bicycles to Belleville. Perhaps Mrs. Wheeler, the Dodges' former landlady, could give them some clues.

"Yes," Nan approved. "Mrs. Wheeler might remember something more about Jimmy's other treasure maps."

The twins asked their mother if they might

make the trip. Mrs. Bobbsey gave permission, saying:

"Be very careful and take Elderberry Road. There isn't much traffic."

Before setting out, Bert and Freddie received phone calls from Charlie and Johnnie. Both boys reported that their parents had signed the letters from Mr. Roland. Also, each wished Jimmy to have his check for taking part in the Horseshoe Island movie.

"Say, that makes it unanimous!" Bert remarked as the four mounted their bicycles.

"U—u—a—nan-i-mous?" Flossie repeated hesitantly.

"Unanimous means we all agree to do the same thing," Nan explained.

Soon the twins were pedaling toward Belleville. They found the ride along Elderberry Road a pleasant one. As Mrs. Bobbsey had said, there were not many automobiles, so the cyclists made good time.

About midmorning they arrived in the small, pretty town of Belleville. Suddenly the twins came to an abrupt halt. They looked at one another sheepishly as the same thought struck them at once.

"Goodness!" Nan exclaimed. "Fine detectives we are! We didn't even get Mrs. Wheeler's address from Jimmy."

"Let's go in that drugstore and look it up in the phone book," Bert said.

The Bobbseys dismounted and parked, then hurried inside the drugstore. Bert consulted the directory and groaned.

"There are four Mrs. Wheelers," he reported.

The twins inquired of the proprietor if he knew a Mrs. Wheeler who rented out apartments.

"Sorry," he replied. "I don't. I'm new here."

"Well," Nan said to the others, "we'll just have to phone all the Wheelers until we find the right one."

Bert pulled some coins from a pocket and went

into the booth. Anxiously his brother and sisters
waited. The first time Bert received no response.
The second number he dialed brought a busy
signal.

The third Mrs. Wheeler answered the phone,
but told Bert she knew no one named Dodge. The
boy had no better luck on his fourth call.

"Maybe," Nan said, "that busy line is free
now."

"You try," her twin suggested.

Nan dialed the number. "It's ringing," she said
after a moment.

Then Nan heard the receiver being lifted
and a high-pitched voice saying, "Hello?
Hello?"

The other Bobbseys listened hopefully as Nan
asked, "Mrs. Wheeler?"

"Yes. Yes I am."

"Are you the Mrs. Wheeler who rented an
apartment to Mrs. Dodge and her grandson—"

"Jimmy?" the woman interrupted. "I should
say so. And I never had such fine tenants, either,
I might add. Both of 'em so brave after poor
Captain Dodge went down with his ship. I was
sure sorry when they moved to Lakeville."

"Lake*port,*" Nan corrected gently. "That's
where I live."

"Oh yes. I'm always getting that name mixed
up," the talkative Mrs. Wheeler replied, then de-

manded rather sharply, "Say, who are you any-way? And why do you want to know about the Dodges?"

Nan had had little chance to state the purpose of her call. But now she quickly gave her name and asked if she and her brothers and sister might call on Mrs. Wheeler.

"We are trying to help the Dodges," Nan explained.

"Oh, if that's the case, come right over, dear. I'm at 26 Oakwood Avenue, two blocks from the center of town."

Nan thanked her and hung up. Bert said with a smile, "I guess you found the right Mrs. Wheeler, sis."

Eagerly the twins left the drugstore and started off on their bicycles. They had no trouble locating Oakwood Avenue and turned into the tree-shaded street.

"There's number 26." Flossie pointed to a white, rambling house with a well-kept yard.

The children rode up the walk, bordered with petunias. They hopped off and propped their bicycles against the side of the porch steps. Just then the door opened, and a plump, white-haired woman came out.

"Hello there," she greeted with a pleasant smile. "I'm Mrs. Wheeler."

Nan stepped forward. "I'm Nan Bobbsey, the girl who talked to you on the phone. And this is my twin, Bert, and our twin brother and sister, Flossie and Freddie."

The woman chuckled. "My, two sets of twins. Well, come right up and sit on the porch where it's nice and cool."

The children took seats in comfortable wicker chairs. As Mrs. Wheeler sat down she said:

"I'm sorry if I sounded suspicious when you asked about the Dodges. But I wanted to be careful, especially since that strange-looking man was here a few days ago asking where they were."

The twins sat bolt upright. "A strange-looking man?" Bert echoed. "Did he have a scar on his cheek, and a black dog with him?"

CHAPTER XV

THE MOVING VAN CLUE

MRS. WHEELER looked at the twins in surprise. "Why, yes. Do you know this scar-faced man?"

"Not exactly," Nan replied. "But we suspect he's been following Jimmy Dodge and watching our house, too."

Quickly Bert told Mrs. Wheeler about first noticing the stranger on the train, and of his actions since that time.

"We believe," he went on, "that this Mr. Scarface has some connection with Jimmy's father and might know something about what happened to him."

"Oh dear," Mrs. Wheeler said in dismay. "I'm afraid I'm responsible for the man being on the same train as Jimmy when he came down from the farm."

Nan requested that she tell the children how it had happened.

Mrs. Wheeler nodded. "He really came here twice," she admitted. "The first time was in the morning. I didn't like him, but when he said he was looking for Captain Dodge he caught me off guard.

"I told him, 'Why, the Captain's been lost at sea, and his family's moved to Lakeville. His son Jimmy is going there on the afternoon train today.' "

The woman paused. "And then?" Nan urged her eagerly.

"I asked the man who he was. But he went off without a word, dragging his dog with him," Mrs. Wheeler recalled with a frown. "An hour later he was back. Told me there wasn't any such town as Lakeville on the railroad timetable."

The house owner sighed. "Of course I'd gotten the name mixed up. So I said to him, 'Oh, I meant Lake*port*. That's not far away from here!' Should've bitten off my tongue."

"Oh, that would hurt," Flossie said seriously.

The woman smiled ruefully. "I mean, I ought not to tell people so much. I'd feel awful if any more trouble comes to the Dodges, just because I'm so scatterbrained."

"Don't worry, Mrs. Wheeler," Nan said. "You may really have helped a lot. If Mr. Scarface was looking for the Captain, perhaps he is still alive."

"I hadn't thought of that," Mrs. Wheeler said. "Though I'm sure Captain Dodge would've contacted his folks by this time. If I see that fellow again, I'll get in touch with you right away."

"Maybe the Captain couldn't find them," Bert suggested. "Where did they live before they came here?"

"On Beech Street. They rented a nice place there, but when the Captain didn't return, they had to give it up. The place has been vacant ever since."

"So there'd be no one to answer a phone call if Captain Dodge called there," Bert remarked.

"But mail should have been forwarded to this address," Nan said.

"The Dodges never got any here from the Captain," Mrs. Wheeler told the twins.

"It's very strange," Nan murmured.

Then she questioned Mrs. Wheeler about Jimmy's missing envelope of maps.

Before she could answer Freddie piped up, "We found one map in a Spanish pirate hat. Flossie said you prob'ly put it in there so the hat wouldn't get smashed."

Mrs. Wheeler thought for a moment. "Yes, that's exactly what I did. It slipped out of the envelope. And not realizing the drawing was of any value, I did stuff it into that fancy hat."

She added, however, that she was certain the

envelope containing the maps had been put into the moving van. "I think it was on top of some books."

The children rose to leave, feeling that they had taken enough of Mrs. Wheeler's time. But she insisted upon serving them milk and cookies.

"You must be hot and thirsty after your long ride," she said.

After the refreshment, the children thanked Mrs. Wheeler and said good-by.

"Remember me to the Dodges," she called as they mounted their bicycles.

Suddenly Bert remembered one more thing he wanted to know. He asked Mrs. Wheeler the name of the company who had taken care of the Dodges' moving.

"Jones and Son on Main Street," was the reply. "It's near the center of town, to the right."

As the cyclists rode off, Nan said to her twin, "You think we might pick up a clue at the mover's?"

"I hope so," Bert replied, "if they'll let us look around."

"Maybe Jimmy's maps got mixed up with somebody else's things," Freddie suggested.

"Could be. We'll see what we can find out."

Arriving at the large building marked Jones & Son Company, the children entered the little office. A man sat at a battered old desk.

"Yes?" he said, as the children came forward. "I'm very busy."

"We're sorry to bother you," Nan spoke up politely. "But we'd like to ask you something important."

"Well, hurry up and tell me what it is," the man said brusquely.

Bert gave their names, then said, "We understand your company did the moving for a Mrs. Dodge from here to Lakeport this summer."

"Dodge? Dodge?" repeated the man. "Now listen here, kids. We move hundreds of people every week. I can't remember all their names."

"Can't you tell from your records?" Nan inquired pleasantly. "You see, sir, Mrs. Dodge's grandson Jimmy, who couldn't come today, lost a Manila envelope with some very valuable maps inside."

"We thought maybe it got stuck in with another person's things," Freddie put in. "We've looked all over for it."

The man threw up his hands. "What'll I hear next!" He glared at the children. "I'm president of this company, and I'll have you know my company is very careful. We *never* get anything mixed up—or lost. But I'll check."

He pulled a big ledger from his desk drawer and consulted it. As he ran one finger down a certain page, he said, "Hmmm-m. Guess this is it. Dodge—from Belleville to Glenwood Place, Lakeport."

"Yes, that's right," Freddie told him.

Bert suddenly had an idea. "Perhaps we could take a look in the van that moved Mrs. Dodge's things."

Mr. Jones looked at him, and even smiled a little. "You kids really want to help your friend Jimmy, don't you?"

"Oh, yes," they chorused.

He glanced at the ledger again. "Let's see. It was van No. 37 that did the job. I'll check and see if it's in the garage."

He pressed his buzzer. "Van 37 in?" he asked someone. "Fine."

"Okay." Mr. Jones got up and led the way outside into a huge garage. "There's van No. 37. Search to your heart's content. I'll be in my office. Let me know what happens."

Eagerly the twins clambered up into the opened back of the van, and walked up and down the large compartment. The children scanned the walls, which were covered with padded cloth.

Freddie stopped and stared around. "It just looks plain empty," he declared, disappointed.

"It does," Bert agreed, "but we won't give up yet."

The children then began feeling the padded covering with their hands. Bert knelt on the floor and examined the slight space between the planks and the padding.

Suddenly his alert eyes spotted a little bulge

below a rip in the cloth. Quickly he reached underneath it. His fingers closed on what felt like heavy paper.

"I've found something!" cried Bert.

CHAPTER XVI

A PUZZLING CALL

BERT drew out the object he had felt underneath the padding. The others had joined him and looked on tensely.

"Oh! Oh!" Flossie squealed the next second. "It's a big brown envelope."

The twins hardly dared hope they had succeeded in solving Jimmy's mystery. Did the bulky envelope Bert held in his hands contain the missing treasure maps?

"Quick, Bert, open it!" Flossie urged.

Carefully her brother pulled out a roll of papers. "There are five," he observed.

"That's how many maps Jimmy lost," Freddie said excitedly.

The twins gave a triumphant shout, as the first paper proved indeed to be a map. It was the outline of an island, accompanied by lists of numbers and symbols.

"The second treasure chart," Nan said happily, seeing the Roman numeral two in the upper left-hand corner.

The twins examined the other parchment sheets and found that they also bore map sketches and code markings.

"And they're numbers three, four, and five," Bert said. "That clinches it."

Exuberantly the Bobbseys jumped from the van compartment and ran into Mr. Jones's office.

"We found Jimmy's maps!" they announced.

The man looked amazed. "You did? They were really in the van?"

Bert explained how they had been wedged into the small space. Mr. Jones gave a broad smile. "Well, next time I won't be so sure we can't make a mistake." He rose and shook hands with each twin. "I'm glad you'll have good news for your pal."

They smiled and thanked him. Then the Bobbseys hastened outside to their bicycles. Bert put the rolled-up maps in the basket of his bicycle, and the four sped off.

"Let's go right to the lumberyard," Freddie urged, "and tell Jimmy."

"You bet!" Bert agreed.

By the time the twins pulled up near their father's office, it was way past lunchtime. But they were so elated by their discovery that even Freddie forgot to be hungry.

To their delight, Jimmy was in Mr. Bobbsey's office about to go on an errand.

"Daddy! Jimmy!" Freddie began. "We—"

But Jimmy had already spotted the roll in Bert's hands. "You found the charts!" he cried out.

Bert handed Jimmy the maps. The boy slowly opened each one. His face grew radiant. "Yes," he said. "These *are* the rest of my treasure maps."

The twins then took turns relating the story of their search. Mr. Bobbsey and Jimmy listened with increasing amazement.

"Oh, I'm so glad to have these back," Jimmy said. "I—I can hardly believe it!"

Bert asked the boy if he had the mysterious partly finished map.

"Yes." Jimmy brought out the crumpled sheet and compared it with his chart for the Pacific island treasure.

"Everything on this paper is exactly the same as on the real map," he announced.

The twins studied Jimmy's chart. "Zowie!" Bert exclaimed. "I'll bet the code for this big treasure is a tough one."

The others agreed, seeing the complicated list of symbols, numbers, and letters.

"Dad said this was the hardest," Jimmy recalled. "If only—" he stopped. For a moment a wistful look came into his eyes.

Nan knew instantly what he was wishing—
that his father could be present. She longed to
tell him of Mr. Scarface's call at Mrs. Wheeler's
asking for Captain Dodge. But until the twins
had found a few more clues, she decided not to
raise Jimmy's hopes needlessly.

Instead Nan merely told him that they had
stopped at Mrs. Wheeler's while on the trail of
the lost maps.

"She was very nice," Nan went on, "and gave
us directions to the mover's."

"And cookies and milk, too," Freddie added,
realizing that right now he was very hungry.

"Mrs. Wheeler always was good to us,"
Jimmy remarked with a smile, "and helped
Grandma a lot. She even went to the post office
to give them our new address when Grandma
moved here."

At this point Mr. Bobbsey suggested that
Jimmy telephone his grandmother at the dress-
making shop.

"I think she'd be happy to hear your latest
news," he said.

Eagerly Jimmy went to do this. While he was
out of the room, the twins quickly told their father of Mr. Scarface's two calls at Mrs. Wheeler's home.

Mr. Bobbsey looked thoughtful. "It certainly
does sound as though this fellow, whoever he is,
knows something about Captain Dodge."

Jimmy returned shortly to report that Mrs. Dodge had been thrilled at the news. "Grandma says the check came from Mr. Roland, and she signed the letter he sent. And *I* feel so good," the boy said with a grin, "I could work like six people!"

"You already do," Mr. Bobbsey praised him with a smile.

The twins left and hurried home to a late lunch. For the remainder of the day, Bert was very quiet. He was mulling over an idea about Captain Dodge's disappearance which had popped into his head. "But it's crazy," he argued with himself. "It couldn't be."

At any rate, Bert resolved to say nothing to the others for the present. "I'll do some investigating first," he determined.

Nan sensed that her twin had something on his mind. Although curious, she refrained from asking questions, knowing Bert was not yet ready to confide in her.

Charlie Mason and Johnnie Wilson stopped during the afternoon to leave their movie checks with the twins to give to Jimmy.

Before leaving for Belleville the next morning, Flossie asked her mother, "May I please be the one to give Jimmy the surprise money for the bank?"

"Yes, dear, if the other children agree."

Flossie ran to her room. She came down with

the little handbag she carried to Sunday school.

"I'll put the checks in this," the little girl explained.

During the station wagon ride to Belleville, Bert had stared out the window. But he hardly noticed the passing scenery. His idea of the day before persisted. Several times he almost revealed it to the others.

"No," he told himself. "I must be sure."

When they reached the outskirts of Belleville, Jimmy remarked, "It seems like a long time since I lived here."

In a few minutes Mrs. Bobbsey parked near the Belleville bank. Flossie opened her handbag and presented the checks to Jimmy.

"All of us would like you to have these for your bank account."

At first Jimmy, overwhelmed, shook his head. "Thank you, but I couldn't take them. You— you've done so much for me already."

Flossie smiled. "We'll be hurt if you don't take them."

Seeing that the twins were firm in their decision, Jimmy accepted the checks.

"This is—" He paused, groping for words. "Well, you're the best friends a fellow could possibly have!"

The whole group went inside the bank, and Mrs. Bobbsey helped Jimmy open a savings ac-

count. The teller handling the transaction looked
at Jimmy and inquired:

"Aren't you the grandson of Mrs. Dodge, who
used to have an account here?"

"Yes," Jimmy replied. "She and I are living
in Lakeport now."

"Oh," said the teller. "I wish I'd known that.
A few days ago we had a long-distance call from

California. Someone was trying to get in touch with your grandmother."

"Who was it?" Jimmy asked in amazement.

"I couldn't catch the man's name. I just about heard him ask for Mrs. Dodge. The connection was very bad. But anyway I did tell him that your grandmother had closed her account here and left no forwarding address. Then the line went dead."

"Did the person ever call back?" Jimmy asked eagerly.

The teller shook his head. "I'm sorry. If I had known it was something important, I would have tried to call the person back."

Jimmy was perplexed. "I'm sure Grandma doesn't know anybody in California. Now who could have called her?"

CHAPTER XVII

CAPTURED!

RETURNING to the station wagon, the Bobbseys and Jimmy puzzled over the bank teller's story. Who could have been trying to reach Mrs. Dodge from the West Coast?

The twins' mother started the car and pulled away from the bank. "Perhaps," she remarked, "if the phone connection was so bad, the teller misunderstood."

Bert meanwhile had come to a decision. "Mother, would you mind stopping at the Belleville post office. I want to ask someone there a question."

"All right." Mrs. Bobbsey was surprised, but sensed that her son had a good reason for making the request.

She parked in front of the post office building, and Bert ran inside. The others waited, their curiosity growing by leaps and bounds.

"I'll bet he's chasing some kind of clue," Nan guessed.

"I hope it's a good one," Flossie said.

Finally Bert emerged from the post office and climbed into the car. There was an air of suppressed excitement about him.

"Did you find out what you wanted?" Nan could not resist asking her twin.

Bert nodded. "Yes. But I don't want to tell anybody yet. I might be wrong." He turned to Jimmy. "If my hunch *is* right, though, it's because of something you told me."

Jimmy was mystified. "Can you just say if your hunch is—is about my father?" he asked eagerly.

"Sort of," Bert admitted. He would give no further hint.

Back in Lakeport once more, Mrs. Bobbsey suggested that they have an early luncheon. "How would you all like to eat at The Kopper Kettle Tea Room?" she asked.

"Oh, yes," the twins chorused.

"They have scrumptious desserts there," Flossie told Jimmy.

"And," Mrs. Bobbsey went on, "I thought we would stop and see if Mrs. Dodge can go with us."

"Goody!" Flossie said. "We'll have an eating-out party."

"Grandma would love that," Jimmy said.

A little later, the Bobbseys and Dodges were seated at a big round table in the Kopper Kettle. Jimmy's dog Laddie had been left at the lumber-yard, which was near the restaurant. Mike would take care of the collie.

With his blue eyes shining, Jimmy now said to his grandmother, "The twins and Sam and Charlie and Johnnie all gave me a wonderful present for my new bank account."

When Mrs. Dodge heard what this was, her eyes grew moist. "Why," she said softly, "you Bobbseys make it seem as if it were Christmas!"

Everyone smiled, and Freddie said, "We like Christmas surprises, too, even in the summer."

During the meal Jimmy asked his grandmother if she knew anyone on the West Coast. He explained about the California phone call received at the Belleville bank.

Mrs. Dodge shook her head, puzzled. "No, I don't know a soul there," she replied.

After dessert had been eaten, Jimmy said, "You were right, Flossie. That was a terrific chocolate nut sundae."

Mrs. Bobbsey paid the check, and the group went outside the restaurant. Mrs. Dodge said, "My, such a lovely treat! Thank you very much."

She had barely finished speaking when a fran-tic barking was heard. The sound came from the direction of the lumberyard.

"It's Laddie!" Jimmy cried out.

"Let's see what's going on!" Freddie urged.

The children ran toward the yard with Mrs. Dodge and Mrs. Bobbsey following. The next moment an astonishing sight met their eyes.

Running directly up the street toward them was the scar-faced man and his black dog!

Racing full-tilt after the man was Laddie. Behind the collie came Mike Donovan.

"We'll catch him!" Bert shouted. "He won't get away this time!"

Staunchly the twins and Jimmy formed a little barricade across the sidewalk. When Mr. Scarface saw them, he stopped in his tracks. He looked wildly in all directions, then darted into the street. Cars screeched to a halt and horns honked loudly. By this time a traffic officer came on the run, attracted by the commotion.

"Catch that man, Mr. Policeman!" Flossie shrieked. "He's trying to take something that doesn't belong to him!"

The officer caught up with the fugitive and seized his arm. He marched the man up to the Bobbseys and the others. A crowd of spectators had gathered.

"You say this fellow's a thief?" demanded the policeman, looking at Flossie.

Before she could explain, Bert stepped forward. "We're not sure that he is. But we suspect that he may have taken something from my father's lumberyard."

"And he's been spying on Jimmy Dodge," Freddie spoke up boldly, "and on our house, too."

The officer kept a firm grip on the prisoner's arm and said, "Oh, I guess you twins are Mr. Richard Bobbsey's children."

"Yes," Mrs. Bobbsey spoke up, "and I am his wife. I believe this man has some explanations to make."

"He sure has," Mike snapped, as Jimmy held onto Laddie. The collie was uttering low growls at the black dog, who had slunk to his master's side.

The lumberyard day watchman explained that he was making his rounds with Laddie when the collie began sniffing the ground and growling.

"It was near the lumber stacks where we found Freddie the other day," Mike continued. "I spotted this fellow snooping around one of the piles. He saw me and zoomed out through the gate."

All this time the prisoner had remained stubbornly silent. Beneath the brim of his felt hat, Mr. Scarface's eyes shifted nervously.

It was decided that they would all go to Mr. Bobbsey's office and interrogate the stranger. The officer and Mike escorted him, while the others went in the station wagon.

Mr. Bobbsey was astounded when his family, the Dodges, Mike, and the policeman with their prisoner crowded into his office.

Breathlessly the twins told their father what had happened.

"And you sit here," the officer ordered Mr. Scarface, placing a chair in the middle of the room.

When the man was seated, Mr. Bobbsey walked over to him. "First of all," said the twins' father sternly, "what is your name?"

The prisoner spoke for the first time. "Carlos Spanandi," he said sullenly.

"And what were you looking for around here and at the Dodges' home and our place?" Mr. Bobbsey pressed.

Carlos Spanandi lapsed into another obstinate silence. He stared at the floor.

Bert came to stand by his father. "Did you want to finish copying the chart Captain Dodge made for his son, and try getting the treasure on the Pacific island for yourself?" the boy asked Spanandi.

The prisoner looked up suddenly. "You found it—I mean—"

He stopped, but everyone could see that Bert's question had struck home.

"Did you once steal the real Pacific island treasure chart from Captain Dodge so you could make one of your own?" Bert prodded.

The policeman commanded, "Answer the boy!"

Finally Carlos Spanandi muttered, "Yes."

"And for some reason you had to return the Captain's chart before you could finish copying it?" Nan put in.

The prisoner nodded slightly. There was an exchange of glances among those in the room. Then Mrs. Dodge voiced the next question uppermost in all their minds.

"Mr. Spanandi, where did you know my son?"

The answer startled everyone.

"I was in the crew of Captain Dodge's ship."

CHAPTER XVIII

A HAPPY SURPRISE

MR. SCARFACE a member of Captain Dodge's crew! Slowly Jimmy asked him:

"Were you aboard the *Flying Dolphin* when it was wrecked near South America?"

Carlos Spanandi nodded. "Yes," he admitted. "I managed to stay afloat until a fisherman's boat rescued me and the other crewmen."

He added that the fishermen had brought them ashore to a small village on the Pacific coast of South America. From there, Spanandi had eventually made his way to California.

"California!" Bert repeated to himself. This might fit in with his idea!

Nan now asked the prisoner, "Did you see what happened to Captain Dodge?"

"I thought I saw him in the water just as the *Dolphin* went under. But in the rain and darkness I could not be certain."

"Then," Mrs. Dodge's voice trembled, "you believe my son, the Captain, was—lost?"

Carlos Spanandi did not answer, but lowered his eyes. Suddenly Bert queried:

"Mr. Spanandi, if you thought Captain Dodge was lost, why did you go to Belleville and ask Mrs. Wheeler where he was?"

The prisoner almost leaped out of his chair at Bert's question, and the Dodges looked startled.

"How did you—?" Carlos Spanandi caught himself and looked around wildly.

The policeman addressed him sternly. "Tell us everything, Spanandi. Withholding information won't do you any good."

The prisoner took a deep breath. "All right," he muttered.

The Bobbseys leaned forward expectantly as Carlos Spanandi spoke.

"I went to Belleville to ask Captain Dodge if he'd help me get another job on a ship." A puzzled expression crossed the man's face. "It is strange you people do not know where the Captain is."

Mrs. Dodge asked haltingly, "You mean that —that you have seen my son alive?"

"Yes."

The single word electrified the entire group. Jimmy demanded tensely, "Where is my father?"

"I saw him a short time ago in California," was the reply.

There was an astounded silence. Finally the police officer thundered, "Spanandi, you'd better be on the level."

"I am not lying," the man insisted. "Unless it was a ghost, I saw Captain Dodge on the West Coast less than two months ago."

"You didn't speak to him?" Nan put in quickly.

The prisoner hesitated, then shook his head. "No. I was down at the waterfront and saw the Captain getting off a freighter that had just docked."

"If you wanted a job on a ship," Bert pressed, "why didn't you ask him then?"

Spanandi shifted uneasily in his chair. Suddenly Freddie burst out, "You really wanted to come to Belleville and get the map away from the Captain again."

"And when you found out he wasn't there," Nan interposed, "you followed Jimmy to Lakeport and watched our house to find out where the chart was."

"That's why you went to Mr. Bobbsey's office," Jimmy accused, "and took his envelope. You thought my map was inside."

Carlos Spanandi stammered, "I—I only wanted to help the Captain—er—dig for the treasure."

"You mean you hoped to decode the map," Bert declared, "and help yourself to the Pacific island treasure."

The prisoner, completely dejected, confessed that this was so. Further questioning revealed that he had hitch-hiked across the country from California. By the time he arrived in Lakeport, his money was almost gone.

Spanandi said that he had spent the rest of his funds on food and taxis to spy on Jimmy and the Bobbseys. He had slept in an abandoned barn just outside Lakeport.

"Every day I kept expecting to see Captain Dodge," he added.

The ex-crewman explained that he had learned of the treasure map aboard the *Flying Dolphin*. "I saw the map on the Captain's desk," he said, "and a letter to his son telling of the hidden treasure."

The prisoner admitted that he had instantly begun copying the chart. But he had heard footsteps approaching and dashed from the cabin with his unfinished sketch. He had noted the Belleville address from Captain Dodge's letter. Also, he had recognized Jimmy on the train from a photograph in the Captain's quarters.

The prisoner hunched his shoulders. "I thought the island treasure would bring me a fortune."

Then the scar-faced man was taken away to the police station by the officer. After they had departed, everyone excitedly discussed Spanandi's startling story.

Jimmy heaved a sigh. "I wish we could find out where Dad is."

Bert, meanwhile, determined to put his idea about the sea captain to a test without further delay. He waited until the others had left the office. Then Bert said to his father:

"Dad, I need your help with some long-distance detective work."

Quickly the boy explained what he had in mind. When he had finished, Mr. Bobbsey remarked, "I think your theory is excellent, son. We won't say a word until we see how it works out. I'll begin checking now." He reached for the telephone.

That evening at supper, Bert excitedly asked, "Any luck, Dad, with your detecting job?"

Mr. Bobbsey answered with a broad smile. "Bert, your idea was a success." He looked around at his family. "I believe we'll soon have a very special surprise for everyone!"

"Oh, boy!" Freddie exclaimed. "When?"

Mr. Bobbsey replied, "Right after lunch tomorrow. Since it's Saturday, I thought the Dodges could go with us for a little drive."

"I'll call them," Nan offered and excused

herself from the table. Returning, she reported
that Jimmy and his grandmother would be glad
to join them.

"Is the ride part of the surprise?" Flossie
wanted to know.

Mr. Bobbsey chuckled. "In a way it is."

"Whatever the secret is," Mrs. Bobbsey said
with a smile, "I'm sure it's a happy one."

The following afternoon the Bobbseys and
Dodges set off in the station wagon. Laddie was
curled at Jimmy's feet. At first Mrs. Dodge
looked pale and sad, but as they left the outskirts
of town her spirits rose a little.

"This is nice," she said. "I haven't seen the
countryside by car for a long time."

Flossie and Freddie had been gazing out the
window, wondering when the surprise would be
revealed. Presently Freddie said:

"Daddy, aren't we going toward the airport?"

"Yes," replied Mr. Bobbsey. Turning his
head a little, he asked, "Would everybody like to
stop there and watch a big cross-country plane
come in? I believe one is due to land shortly."

His passengers readily agreed, and Mr. Bobbsey drove on to the air terminal building. He
parked nearby, and the group went inside the
terminal. Jimmy held Laddie by his leash.

As they entered, a voice came over the loud-
speaker. "Announcing Flight Number 452 from
San Francisco."

Bert said eagerly, "That must be the big plane now."

His father nodded, and everyone went over to the gate. Pretty soon the Bobbseys and their friends could see the huge silver aircraft touch down at the far end of the field. It taxied to a gentle standstill.

The landing ramp was rolled up, and the passengers began disembarking. Nan noticed that her twin had become very quiet and was watching the plane intently. At the same moment she heard Jimmy catch his breath.

Nan observed that he was staring at a tall, fine-looking man who had just come down the ramp from the aircraft. Suddenly a shout of joy burst from Jimmy's lips. "Dad! *Dad!*"

The next instant Mrs. Dodge cried out, "Henry, my son! Oh, it's too good to be true!"

As the tall man approached, Bert and his father beamed. The other Bobbseys were speechless with amazement. Finally Nan gasped, "Why, Bert! What a wonderful, *wonderful* surprise!"

The Captain strode through the gate, and in a second the three Dodges were exchanging hugs and kisses, while Laddie barked excitedly. Then, his face radiant, Jimmy introduced his father to the Bobbseys.

"If I had all the gold in the world," the Captain said in a voice deep with emotion, "it wouldn't repay you Bobbseys for reuniting me with my mother and my son."

"We're awfully glad you're here," Flossie spoke up, "and not shipwrecked any more."

"This is the happiest day of my life," declared Mrs. Dodge with shining eyes.

The twins' mother smiled. "I suggest we go back to our house and hear the Captain's story."

Eagerly the group hurried to the station wagon and returned to Lakeport. At the Bobbsey house, Dinah and Sam welcomed Captain Dodge in astonished delight. Snap and Snoop, sensing the excitement, frisked about with Laddie.

As soon as the Bobbseys and their friends were seated in the living room, Jimmy begged, "Please tell us everything that happened, Dad!"

The Captain gave Laddie a pat, then began, "I'll start at the end of my story, so to speak. When Mr. Bobbsey reached me by phone in California, I was just about to leave a hospital."

"Hospital!" echoed Mrs. Dodge.

"Don't worry," her son assured her. "I'm fine now. Nothing worse than a broken leg. The day I arrived in California, a thick fog descended. You couldn't see even inches ahead. I misjudged a high curb and fell, fracturing a leg bone. So off to the hospital I went."

Captain Dodge continued, "Being laid up was a blow to me. Nevertheless I kept sending letters and cables home, as I had done from the freighter which brought me to California. But eventually they all came back marked, 'No such street address.' "

Jimmy and his grandmother looked puzzled. "How strange," Mrs. Dodge remarked. "The Belleville post office had our new address."

The Captain smiled ruefully. "Not quite. Bert found out that on their records it said Lakeville instead of Lakeport."

Freddie turned to his brother and asked, "Is that why you went to the post office?"

"Yes," replied Bert and added, "Jimmy gave me the idea there might be a mix-up when he said Mrs. Wheeler gave the Dodges' address to the post office. I remembered how she kept getting the name of our town wrong."

Nan glanced at her twin admiringly. "You were smart to figure that out."

Captain Dodge explained that the telephone call to Mrs. Dodge at the bank had been from a doctor at the hospital.

"I requested the doctor to try contacting Mother," the Captain went on, "since I was still unable to walk at the time. But there was a violent thunderstorm during the doctor's call. Before he could explain fully to the bank, the lines were struck by lightning and put out of use for several days."

Smiling at the twins, the Captain said, "Your father told me about that scoundrel Spanandi. He was not a very reliable worker aboard ship, but I never suspected he wanted Jimmy's map and planned to find the Pacific island treasure himself."

"Anyhow," Captain Dodge went on, "Spanandi did us one favor. It was through his admission of having seen me on the Coast that Bert guessed why I hadn't returned to this area—that possibly I was in a hospital."

Flossie spoke up. "And our daddy called up

all the hospitals out there till he found the right one."

"Exactly," the Captain said. "Otherwise, it might have taken me a long time to locate my family."

"Aren't the twins great?" Jimmy exclaimed. "They found you, Dad, and the treasure charts, and helped me find my seventh birthday treasure, the one you hid on Horseshoe Island."

It was the Captain's turn to be amazed as he heard for the first time the details of all the children's recent adventures.

"I certainly hope," he said to the twins, "that you and your two friends will go with Jimmy and me to search for his second island treasure."

"We'd love to," Nan responded.

Then Freddie pleaded, "Captain Dodge, please tell us about the wreck of the *Flying Dolphin!*"

A hush fell over the room as Jimmy's father began, "We were steaming along the coast of Chile, when a violent gale came up. Suddenly a gigantic wave smashed the *Dolphin* and broke her in half. The next thing I knew, I was struggling in the raging waters.

"My chances looked slim, but luckily a lifeboat from the *Dolphin* floated by, and I managed to climb in. Somehow I rode out the gale and began rowing."

The Captain had found emergency rations on the lifeboat. But after days of rowing on the open sea, his strength had ebbed and the supplies had almost given out. Finally he had sighted a tiny island.

"I headed for shore," he continued. "The lifeboat, though, was torn apart on the reefs. I swam the rest of the way."

The island, explained the Captain, was one of many along South America's Pacific Coast. It was uninhabited and isolated, but at least had several fruit trees and edible plants.

Captain Dodge sighed. "I thought I'd be there forever. I soon realized the island must be outside the regular ship routes. Weeks and months went by, until one day I did see a freighter passing by. I signaled frantically. Finally the crew spotted me and picked me up. The ship stopped at many ports to deliver cargo, so it took several months to reach the West Coast. The rest of my story you know," he concluded.

"Wow! What an ocean trip!" exclaimed Freddie. "Did you find any pirates' gold while you were on the island?"

"No. But," the Captain's eyes twinkled, "I did find another kind of valuable treasure from the oysters there."

He reached into his jacket pocket and pulled out a small box. Opening it, he displayed the contents.

"Oo-oo!" Flossie's eyes grew wide. "What bee-yoo-tiful pearls!"

Nestled in the box were about two dozen of the shimmering, lustrous gems. "These," said the Captain, "will go toward a new home for us. Also, they'll help finance our future trip to the Pacific island where Jimmy's last treasure is buried."

"Henry, how wonderful!" exclaimed Mrs. Dodge.

Captain Dodge then insisted on presenting a gift to each of the twins. "A small token of appreciation to Jimmy's loyal and generous friends," he added.

Nan and Flossie were thrilled when he presented both with a pearl. To Bert he gave a bone-handled penknife.

"Thanks a lot, sir," said Bert. "This is keen!"

The Captain turned to Freddie. With a chuckle, he asked the little boy, "Would you like to have the model of the old Spanish galleon?"

"Oh, yes!" Freddie cried in delight. "I won't have to build one now."

At that moment the phone rang. Bert went to answer it. In a few minutes he returned, grinning, and announced that the caller had been Mr. Roland, the movie director.

"Mr. Roland says 'Captain Jimmy's Island Treasure' is playing at the movies tonight," Bert reported. "He hopes all the performers and their families can be there."

"Goody!" Flossie exclaimed, and Nan asked, "Captain Dodge, can you come to see us all in Jimmy's moving picture?"

"I wouldn't miss it for anything," was the hearty reply.

"Also," Bert went on, "Mr. Roland would like Jimmy to make a little speech about the movie before it starts."

"I know what I'll say first," Jimmy declared promptly. "I'll say: 'This motion picture is dedicated to the best detective team I know—the Bobbsey Twins.'"